CYNTHIA HICKEY

WARRING WITH LOVE

Finding Love the Harvey Girl Way
Book 4

Cynthia Hickey

Copyright © **2015**
Written by: Cynthia Hickey
Published by: Winged Publications
Cover Design: Cynthia Hickey

This book is a work of fiction. Names, characters, places, and incidents are the product of the author's imagination and are used fictitiously. Any resemblance to actual events, locales, or persons, living or dead, is coincidental.

No part of this book may be copied or distributed without the author's consent.

All rights reserved.

ISBN-13: **979-8-8690-9044-7**

DEDICATION

As always, to my husband, Tom, and to God. Both who never give up on me..

Trust in the Lord and do good; dwell in the land and enjoy safe pasture. Take delight in the Lord, and he will give you the desires of your heart. Commit your way to the Lord; trust in him and he will do this..

-Psalms 37:3-5

WARRING WITH LOVE

1

Betsy Colter stared out the train window, refusing to imagine her ex-fiancé Lloyd's face reflected in the glass. Night fell, leaving the world outside in darkness except for lamps illuminating the train platform. Oh, she shouldn't be so melancholy. She'd discovered weeks ago that her heart wasn't as broken as she'd originally believed. Lloyd never did make her pulse race or mouth go dry. He was just...Lloyd, the boy who'd always been there.

She sighed. Well, no more. Now, he belonged to another, and Betsy sat on a Santa Fe railroad train heading from Kansas City, Kansas, to Colorado Springs, Colorado. Or at least she would be once the train started moving again.

Why not venture out and see what the country might have to offer? Her parents were gone. Father had died five years ago from an accident at the mill and her mother only a few months ago from a car accident. As an only child, Betsy had no one to talk to about the path her future should take. She made her own choices, following God's lead the best she could, and tried to keep loneliness at bay. And now, in her purse sat a contract. She was going to be a Harvey Girl.

With the war in full swing, the Harvey Company had warned her she'd work to the point of exhaustion every day, serving food to thousands of military men each week not only on the arriving trains, but also from nearby Camp Carson. Perfect. Busyness would keep the pain of rejection away. She'd further serve in some other capacity come her day off each week. Whatever it took to make her feel needed again.

Blinking away tears, she rubbed the condensation from her breath off the window and gazed out at the large group of men in army uniforms who congregated on the platform. Several of the men whistled and waved. She smiled and gave a small wave in return. They weren't the first group she'd shared a car with, but they were definitely the largest. She glanced around the train car at the few women onboard. They'd be overrun for sure.

Before she was able to get up, she found herself boxed in by three rowdy young enlisted men.

"Someone beautiful to pass the time with." A private with hair so blond as to be almost white sat across from her.

Next to him sat an olive-skinned young man. The third man plopped next to her, laying his arm casually across the back of the seat and dropping a harmonica into his front pocket.

Betsy straightened and moved as close to the window as possible. Despite not knowing the soldiers, she didn't feel unsafe or uncomfortable, just squished. After all, these would be the type of men she'd serve meals to each day. She could use the train ride to practice her skills at being friendly, yet able to keep the men at arm's length.

"I'm Private First Class Gregory," the man next to her said. "I'm a doctor. You can call me Spencer."

Betsy looked up into eyes the color of a summer sky. His oak-brown hair, even cut as short as was required by the army, gleamed with health. A chiseled jaw and well-defined lips completed the picture. Betsy smiled.

Here was the diversion she needed. Private Gregory's good looks were as far from Lloyd's red hair and freckles as they could possibly be. She held out her hand. "Betsy Colter, Harvey Girl."

"Pleased to meet you. These gentlemen are Private Shuman and Private Perez. We're on the last leg of our journey until we go overseas. Medics, all three of us, reporting to Camp Carson for a few days before heading for France." He flashed her a dimpled grin. "Off to save the world."

"How commendable." The opportunity to enjoy a handsome man's company, knowing she would never see him again, gave Betsy a freedom she didn't think possible. No commitments, no promises to be broken, nothing but good conversation and a few laughs. One of Lloyd's excuses for betraying her was his assertion that all army men were scoundrels—and he hadn't been able to resist the charms of a particular beauty. Betsy's eyes were now wide open. She wouldn't get too attached to any military man, but she didn't mind the attention now and again, same as any other girl.

As the train pulled away from the depot, a waitress in a starched white dress and apron wheeled a cart down the aisle and handed out brown meal boxes.

Private Shuman frowned. "Boxed meals?" He peered after the waitress. "Someone told me the Harvey Company was a classy joint. She looks like a nurse."

"The war has changed a lot of things, Private. This is better fare than the norm, I guarantee you." Betsy opened her box. A fresh turkey sandwich nestled at the bottom with fried potatoes and an apple. Sufficient, even if it wasn't the glamorous meal once served by

Harvey Girls on the trains. She did look like a nurse. Would Betsy serve on the train or in one of the Fred Harvey restaurants?

After a quick prayer of thanksgiving, she bit into her sandwich. The Harvey Girls ministered with smiles and good food rather than medicine. Maybe Betsy had found her place to be needed, and wanted, after all.

"I'm going fishing with those other dames. This gal's already rationed by Gregory." Private Shuman closed his box. "Come on, Perez. If we're quick, we'll beat those guys to the other pretty girls."

Hmmm. Betsy concentrated on her food. The anonymity of being in a crowd was lost now that the intense gaze of Private First Class Gregory focused on her. Why, the man hardly blinked. Whatever could be going on inside his head?

*

The lovely Betsy squirmed under Spencer's study. Her blue eyes looked as if she'd just woken, and the auburn curls clipped back from an oval face made quite the pretty picture. His gaze settled on her lips, the bottom a bit larger than the top. She seemed friendly enough, more than willing to carry on a conversation among a group, but now that it was just the two of them, a shadow crossed her features, and she suddenly found the contents of her meal box more fascinating than him.

"So, where are you from, Betsy?" Spencer wadded up his napkin and tossed it in his box. They had a long night ahead of them, and he couldn't think of a more pleasant way of passing the hours than in the company of a pretty gal.

"Missouri. You?"

"I'm from a small town in the mountains north of Colorado Springs. I'm hoping to squeeze in a visit with my family during my few days at Camp Carson. I know my mother will be pleased." More than pleased, if he were honest. She'd been almost inconsolable when he'd told her of his plans to join the army. Dad had returned from the Great War with an injury that left him with a limp, and Mom worried Spencer would suffer the same fate or worse.

But Mom always said God looked out for His children. Spencer counted on her prayers covering him. Besides, he wasn't going to shoot, but rather save lives with his training as a medic.

"Why did you want to be a Harvey Girl?" He moved to the seat across from her in order to watch her better. "There must have been easier jobs available."

"Why not?" She shrugged. "It pays well, provides me with room and board, and I can serve my country by serving its fighting men."

"Not looking to hitch up with anyone?"

"Get married?" She shook her head. "No, I almost tried that once. It didn't work out." She looked sad and glanced out the window.

Spencer felt like a cad for bringing up the subject, no matter how innocent his question had been. He leaned over and patted her hand. "I'm sorry. I tend to flap my lips without thinking sometimes."

"It's all right." She turned with a smile. "Do you have a girl back home?"

"No one special." It was a good thing, considering the uncertainty that went along with war. "But I see a girl I'd like to write to while I'm away." He winked.

Her cheeks darkened. "I suppose I could accommodate you. Anything to bolster a soldier's spirit." After digging in her purse for a piece of paper, she scribbled the address of the Harvey House in Colorado Springs and handed it to him.

"That's the ticket." He leaned back in his seat and propped his feet on the seat across from him. It would have been nice to have a berth to stretch out in, but everyone made sacrifices during wartime. "Maybe I'll see you again before I leave."

The other soldiers whooped and hollered at the back

of the car. Even with the sounds of a party, and the occasional giggle of one of the other women, he preferred the cozy quiet of time spent in Betsy's company. There was something girl-next-door and wholesome about her that drew him.

Sure it was nice having the attention of girls fluttering around him because of his uniform, but when the lights came down and night fell, it was a nice girl like Betsy that a man craved. Would she let him kiss her? He knew he was being presumptuous, but it was wartime. His gaze settled on her lips again.

The waitress came back down the aisle collecting garbage before the lights dimmed in the railroad car. Lucky soldiers paired up with girls willing to cuddle away the night. Low murmurs and the occasional giggle filled the air.

Spencer slumped farther in his seat. Betsy didn't seem the type of girl who would welcome any physical contact with a man she barely knew. He'd be content to watch her. Her lids drooped until she fell asleep, her head propped against the window glass.

Smiling, Spencer moved beside her and pulled her over to rest on his shoulder. He laid his cheek on the top of her head and breathed in the delicate scent of roses. He sighed and closed his eyes.

The sun streaming through the window woke him. His shoulder felt light. He glanced at the other seat at the red face of Betsy and grinned. "Sleep well?"

"Well enough. You have a very hard shoulder." The corners of her mouth twitched. "Forgive me for using you as a pillow."

He groaned and stretched, trying to pop the kinks out of his back. "Definitely my pleasure."

The train slowed, signaling their arrival in Colorado Springs. Spencer sighed again. Even good things had to end. "May I escort you off the train, Betsy?" Anything to prolong their time together.

"Yes," she answered softly, her eyes fluttering. Not

flirtatious, but enough to let Spencer know he affected her as much as she did him.

He stood and offered her a hand up. All too soon they stood in the crisp autumn air on the train platform. "May I have something of yours to take into battle with me? Something to remind me of the beauty of home?"

"A lock of my hair, perhaps?" She giggled. "Aren't mementos old-fashioned?"

"I'm an old-fashioned kind of guy. Please?"

She thought for a moment. "I have just the thing." She dug in her purse and pulled out a pink handkerchief and a small bottle of toilet water. After giving the small square of fabric a few spritzes of fragrance, she handed it to him. "Every whiff will remind you of me."

"I'm counting on it." He lifted it to his nose and inhaled. "Write regularly?"

"As often as I can." She tilted her head. "But I expect answers in return."

"You'll get them. There's one more thing I require." He cupped her face and lowered his lips to hers.

2

Betsy slipped Spencer's latest letter into her pocket, then headed to the kitchen for a tray of glasses. The letter was dated over a month ago—three months after Spencer had shipped off, and just after they'd met. She shook off the desire to reread his words. The sun may not have made its morning appearance yet, but the soldiers soon would, and they'd be hungry for food and a smile.

"Good morning, Betsy." The head waitress, Gloria, a woman in her forties with a wide smile and dark hair, sailed by like a ship on calm seas. Somehow, she never seemed ruffled no matter how many boisterous soldiers filled the restaurant. "Had any marriage proposals today?" The woman chuckled and pushed through the swinging doors that led to the dining room.

"No, not yet," Betsy muttered. Not a day passed that she didn't receive at least one. They were from lonely souls who wanted to marry that very minute and have someone waiting for them when they returned. That someone wasn't Betsy.

Spencer was different. While she worried about him in the line of duty, he was a world away and not a lot of danger to her emotions.

At least, those were the lies she told herself. Every word he wrote sent her emotions whirling. His letters were so open, so honest, she couldn't help but feel as if he sat there next to her in person, telling her of his trials and victories. What if the lack of a new letter meant he'd found another pen pal? She hoped not. Spencer had come to mean more to her than she'd thought an army man could.

The other soldiers' quick declarations of love only reinforced her opinion of most unmarried military men. Some of the women were just as bad. They thought nothing of saying yes to a man being shipped out. After all, if the man should be killed, the wife was left with a military pension. Was that why Lloyd's new wife had said yes while he was still engaged to Betsy? Or had Lloyd duped her, not letting her know he had a fiancée waiting at home?

The letter crackled in her pocket. How many girls did Spencer trade letters with? Betsy didn't want to know. She refused to think he toyed with her affections. Another betrayal would crush her. She loved receiving his letters full of encouragement and tidbits of the humorous antics from his fellow military men. And she'd even grown used to overlooking the black lines censoring portions of his letters—parts she supposed might be dangerous for her to know about.

What she hadn't gotten used to was the way her heart skipped whenever she saw he'd answered one of her letters, or the eager way her hands shook as she opened it. If she weren't careful, she'd fail to keep her resolve to not get romantically attached to a man in the armed forces, especially one she knew so little about. They'd been corresponding for months and yet Betsy looked forward to each letter as if it were the first one.

Tray of clean glasses and a full pitcher in hand, Betsy made her way to the dining room. She glanced at the wall at a framed photograph of women in stockings and neat uniforms, standing by round tables adorned with white tablecloths and crystal. She began setting the glasses on waiting tables. No round tables with crystal glasses here. Instead, long rectangular tables with as many chairs as possible down each side stretched across the room. The trains arrived full and accommodations had to be made. Things weren't the same as they were before the Depression and the war. The restaurant still held the same excellence of service the Fred Harvey Company always prided itself on. Things only looked different.

The train whistle blew, and the room flew into action. Betsy tucked an errant curl under a hairpin, pasted a smile on her face, and stood at attention ready to welcome whichever branch of the service blew in that day. Most often it was the army, but occasionally they'd get fly boys or Allied troops. Betsy smiled at hearing a French accent. She had a soft spot for the beautiful language of love.

"Bonjour." She poured water for each of the men seated at her section of the table. "What can I get for you gentlemen?"

"Crab soup?" A young man barely out of short pants arched his eyebrows in question.

"I'm sorry, but we don't have crab soup." They'd never had it on the menu, as far as Betsy knew. "We have a great potato soup, though."

"Please, check with your chef." He smiled and waved a hand toward the kitchen. "We will want six."

"Yes, sir." Since when did customers request something not on the menu? When she'd finished with their drinks, Betsy hurried to the kitchen. "We have an order for crab soup. Do we have that?"

The cook, a portly man in his fifties, nodded. "Not yet, but we can. Tell them fifteen minutes."

"The customers can request anything?" What service! For at least the thousandth time in the past four months of working, pride flooded Betsy. Working for the Harvey Company was a true treasure as far as jobs went.

"For our fighting men, yes." Chef Hooper waved a wooden spoon. "If it is in my power to give it to them, they shall have it."

Betsy rushed outside to deliver the good news to the soldiers. A cheer went up at her words, the Frenchmen's joy overflowing at her ability to grant them a simple desire. Her satisfaction at a job well done had not dissipated by the day's end. She'd given each soldier a good meal and a warm smile.

Back and feet aching, Betsy climbed the stairs to the room she shared with two other waitresses. Thankfully, neither had returned from work and Betsy had a few moments of peace in which to reread her letter from Spencer.

> Dear Betsy,
> Three months is too long not to see your beautiful face. Every day I take out your handkerchief. I swear I can still smell the fragrance. I'd love to tell you what part of this beautiful world I'm in right now, but if I did, you'd get more black lines than words after the censors got finished.
>
> I'm happy that you are enjoying your job so much, but I am sorry it is so demanding on you physically. Hang in there, and when I'm on leave, I'll take you on a picnic to rest your weary soul. See how poetic I can be when writing to you? You bring out the best in me.
>
> Continue your prayers for me. Since I'm still in good health, they must be working. Oh, and here is a picture of my

ugly mug in uniform.
All my affection,
Spencer Gregory

Betsy kissed the letter, then carefully refolded it and slid it in her drawer under her extra socks. She ran her finger over the photograph, imagining she could feel his face. She'd frame the picture and set it on her nightstand. She'd also sleep better that night knowing that at the time of penning his words to her, Spencer was alive and well. Should his letters ever stop, she feared she'd think the worst.

When Lloyd's letters had quit arriving, it was because he'd married someone else. As long as Spencer's letters arrived with regularity, Betsy's heart would stay where it belonged. Not that he owed her his affection—not at all. She would simply miss him should the war take him away from her.

> Dearest Spencer,
> Colorado Springs grows quite chilly in the fall, doesn't it? Of course, the cooler weather is a blessing when one is tired from working twelve hours a day; it is nice not to be drenched in perspiration.
>
> The other day, the restaurant manager ordered all the tables pushed to the sides of the dining room and threw an impromptu dance for the train of soldiers passing through. I believe someone was going home and wanted to celebrate. How I wished one of them would have been you. While I pray for your safety every night, I miss my dear friend.

*

Spencer wished he had been at the party, too. Other than Betsy's letters, which arrived in bundles rather than one each day, there was little joy on the battlefields of France. Day after day, he sewed up gashes, repaired wounds or sent those he couldn't help to hospitals in England. So much for staying on the safe side of the line, as he'd promised his mother. More and more often he dodged bullets while going after fallen comrades because they were short on combat medics.

"Another letter from your gal?" His bunkmate Rochester plopped on his cot and undid the laces on his boots. "She must write you every day."

"I believe she does." Spencer folded the letter and tucked it into a pocket of his duffel bag. He'd finish reading it later when he was alone. "I'm not sure how I could manage without her letters."

"I've got a *couple* of fine girls sending me letters. Makes the fighting almost worth it, doesn't it?" Rochester set in boots in a line at the foot of his cot. "Knowing why we fight? That there are gorgeous gals ready to welcome us home? That we're fighting for love and honor?" He lay back on his bed. "Yep, I couldn't do it otherwise."

"I wish I had a walkie-talkie that would reach to Colorado so I could hear her voice. She has the softest, most soothing voice." Spencer shoved his arms into his jacket. Rochester might have time for a rest, but Spencer's shift was just beginning.

"See you later, Doc. Go save some lives." Rochester closed his eyes and rolled over.

Spencer hoped to do just that. He quick-walked to the mess tent. It didn't matter what they served for supper that night, he didn't like working on an empty stomach.

"Hey, Doc." One of the cooks slopped a spoonful of corned beef hash and mashed potatoes onto a tray and handed it to Spencer. "Not much, but it'll fill the hole in your stomach."

"True enough." Spencer stared at the unappetizing mess on his plate before scanning the tent for an empty seat. Finding one, he sat and quickly wolfed down his food. Time was of the essence, always, and no one had the luxury of dawdling over a meal, especially a doctor. They never knew when casualties and injuries would arrive.

The roar of a jeep engine, and the shouts of soldiers, warned him of incoming casualties. He shoved aside his tray and bolted to his feet, calling for the other medical personnel to step it lively.

Outside, he held his arm across his face in an attempt to keep dirt and gravel from pelting him by a fierce wind. It did little good. By the time he made it to the jeep, he'd been peppered with everything from sand to rocks. He spit dirt.

"What do we have?" He called to the driver.

"Multiple gunshot wounds. This one—" the pilot pointed to the nearest soldier strapped on gurney "—is bleeding profusely from a wound to his neck. I'd say he's probably the worst off. They've all been shot, but none are missing any limbs."

"Get him inside!" Spencer waved to two privates and then sprinted to the medical tent.

Inside, he helped lift the injured man to a bed. He scowled at the blood-soaked bandage around the man's neck. "He's lucky to be alive. Looks like the bullet nicked his artery." Slowly, piece by piece, Spencer unwound the bandage from the wound. Someone had done a nice job of taping extra bandages to his wound with enough pressure to stop the rush of blood gushing from his neck.

"It's all right, soldier. We'll fix you up fine and dandy." Spencer patted his shoulder.

The man's eyes popped open. He followed Spencer's movements with quick, furtive glances, then tried to rise.

"Relax." Spencer applied a firmer grip to the man's upper body. "I need some help over here."

The man muttered something.

Spencer leaned closer. Was he speaking...German? No, he wore the uniform of the United States. "What's going on here?" He stepped back. "Are you an imposter?"

The man lunged, knocking Spencer backward into the tray of surgical equipment. The German grabbed a scalpel and waved it toward Spencer's face, yelling in the language of the enemy.

"Someone shoot him!" Spencer aimed a punch for the man's jaw and missed. His foot slipped in the blood on the floor. He regained his footing and narrowed his eyes. "How did you get that uniform? Who did you have to kill to steal it?" And where was Spencer's help? He glanced around the empty tent as he reached for the pistol at his waist. The others hadn't returned yet. All he needed to do was distract the madman in front of him until help arrived.

He put up his hands. "Calm down, soldier. We'll still help you." Then it would be straight to a POW camp.

A private rushed into the tent, gun drawn. "Hey, you!"

The imposter lunged, knocking the gun from Spencer's grasp. He fell on it and scrambled to his feet with Spencer's weapon aimed at the young soldier, the scalpel still in his other hand.

Spencer dove forward.

The man stabbed, slicing a path along Spencer's rib cage.

Spencer fell back, slipping, his side on fire. The corner of a metal desk rushed up to meet him as two more soldiers rushed his assailant. Spencer put out his hands to catch his fall, and failed. The last thing he saw before the darkness took over was the memory of Betsy's smiling face and the disgrace that he could die from simple contact with a piece of furniture.

3

"Good morning."

Spencer turned his head toward the nurse's voice. "How long have I been here?"

"A month. Your coma lasted longer than we'd anticipated, but your vital signs are all good." The rattle of the metal bedside table alerted him to the fact it was supper time. "Roast beef is on the plate at one o'clock, potatoes at six, and green beans at nine. How many fingers am I holding up?"

"Two."

"You can see?"

He gave a sarcastic laugh. "I guessed." He struggled to a sitting position. He couldn't make out anything but dark shadows. Why couldn't he see? "I want to speak with the doctor."

"He's making his rounds. You'll see him shortly." She plumped a pillow and placed it behind him. "You're shipping home tomorrow, lucky you. Is there someone you would like me to contact?"

Betsy came to mind first, but he tossed that idea away. Being the sweet woman she was, she'd want to care for him, and that was something he couldn't stomach. Nor did he want his mother to know how right her fears about him going to war were. "No, there's no one." Better to let him arrive unannounced then have others in a frenzy wondering ahead of time how to care for an invalid who couldn't see his hand in front of his face.

Turning his head, he listened as the nurse padded away in soft-soled shoes. He lay there and waited for the doctor, letting his dinner grow cold. He had nothing to be thankful for. Serving his country, and for what? To be cast off and sent home without time to heal. Spencer was a doctor. He knew the odds of regaining his full sight were next to nothing, but he'd heard stories of restored sight, miracles. The first time he'd opened his eyes all he saw was darkness. Now, a few weeks later, he saw shadows. He punched his mattress. All he needed was time!

"Private First Class Gregory? I'm Doctor McGovern. How are you today?"

"Took you long enough." Spencer turned toward the voice, hating the petulance in his own, but as likely of holding back the words as a broken dam holding back flood waters.

"Lots of men worse off than you, soldier."

"I'm not a soldier. What happened to me? What happened to the German spy?"

"Best witnesses could tell me was that your temple and the corner of an operating table came to meet." The doctor shined a light in his eyes. A flash of his features came into focus, then faded. "Other than the loss of your eyesight, there's nothing wrong with you, physically. The coma had us worried for a while, but sometimes the body knows best what it needs to heal. I don't know what happened to the German."

"I'd say the loss of my eyesight is a lot, being on this

side of the blindness." Spencer shook his head. What kind of a man was he to let the loss of his sight take away his manhood? A weak one. One no longer good for anyone. "Heard I'm being sent home. Why can't you give me time to see? I've improved to seeing shadows. Let me stay until I'm healed."

"That's good news. God willing, you'll make a complete recovery, but we need the bed, son." The doctor clapped his shoulder. "Simple as that. You should be sitting under your own roof in a week's time. You'll be under the supervision of a doctor at Camp Carson. Let's get you out of that bed."

God willing? Had God been so willing, Spencer wouldn't be fighting blindness and a headache that sent shards of pain through his skull every time he turned his head.

Within seconds, he found himself standing and being led by a girl that smelled of fresh flowers. Maybe it was the same nurse who'd served him the meal he didn't eat, or it could be another. He didn't know or care. All he wanted was to wallow in his self-pity, not stumble along the hospital corridor like a ninety-year-old man.

"There are a few more soldiers going home," she said. "Doctor commissioned one of them to watch over you on the trip."

"Now I've been assigned a babysitter?"

She giggled. "It's not a babysitter unless you continue to act like a baby." They stopped, and he felt her turn toward him. "Pardon my frankness, but there are men going home missing limbs. Others that are horribly disfigured. I realize it is traumatic to lose your sight, but you aren't going home in a coffin or missing body parts. You should be thankful."

"Take me back to my bed. We're done here." No slip of a girl had the right to lecture him.

"As you wish." She steered him back. "I'll let you settle yourself in, since you'll be needing to learn how to function on your own. Have a good evening."

Spencer stood beside his bed, or at least where he thought his bed was. How dare she disappear and leave him? He'd have her credentials. He backed up until his knees buckled against the mattress. He turned, barely able to make out the white of the sheets against the black of the surrounding shadows. Great. He'd insist that everyone around him wear nothing but stark white.

He felt along the blankets until he found the top of the sheet. He pulled it down and climbed into bed, tangling the sheet around his legs when he tried pulling it back into place. Frustrated, he fell back, hitting his head against the headboard.

A chuckle came from a nearby patient. "Pull your legs up to your chest, grab the blanket, then slide your legs down while feeling with your toes."

"Thanks." Spencer followed the man's directions and soon found himself under the covers with a pounding headache.

"I'm Private Benson, and I'll be escorting you home."

"Lucky you. Why are you being sent back?"

"Lost my legs when I stepped on a landmine. You may be going home blinded, but at least you'll be walking. Oh, and you'll be pushing my wheelchair. You'll be my legs, and I'll be your eyes."

Spencer groaned and closed his eyes.

*

Betsy wiped the tears from her face when the postman passed by without leaving another letter for her. Well, she'd known it would happen sooner or later. Spencer's correspondence to her would stop. *Please, Lord, let it be because he'd found someone else and not because You've decided to take Him home.* How would she know? She'd live the rest of her life possibly never knowing what had happened to him.

"Chin up." Gloria set a tray of napkin wrapped silverware on the counter. "He'll write."

"No, he might not." She sniffed. "And no one knows

to tell me if anything happened to him."

"Sure they do. I bet he's talked about you to more than one of his buddies. Soldiers stick together, my dear." Gloria peered into her face. "One of them would send a telegram or look you up. Mark my words, you'll discover the fate of your man, good or bad."

"Tomorrow is my day off." Betsy lifted a load of freshly washed linens. "I need something to do to take my mind off waiting for a letter."

"Not sure how you feel about the Germans," Gloria said, a worried look in her eyes, "But the POW camp is looking for volunteers to write for and read to the prisoners, run errands, stuff like that. If you choose to fill your free time that way, expect some flack from folks."

"I could do that."

From what she knew had happened to her grandfather, she felt she could work to prevent another prisoner of war from suffering the same fate. Volunteering was perfect for her. After all, those individual men were not much different from the American soldiers. God cared about men on both sides of the war. She could deal with any snide remarks the other waitresses dished out.

The ever present train whistle blew, signaling the arrival of yet another train of soldiers. Betsy hurried to put the linens in the closet before taking her place in the dining room. She scanned the faces of the men crowding through the doors. She refused to give up hope that one day she'd see Spencer sail through them, dimpled grin directed her way. Maybe love with a soldier was something she refused to dwell on, but the lack of communication with him left a gaping wound in her heart.

"You're a sight for sore eyes." One soldier took her hand while she poured his water. "Sit and talk a spell?"

Betsy cocked her head, keeping her smile in place. "And deprive the other men of my wonderful presence?

You are greedy, sir."

"Yes, I am." He laughed, flashing white teeth as he bit into a slice of fresh bread. "It's women like you that we're fighting for, you know. The pretty faces at home."

Her heart softened. "That is the sweetest thing anyone has ever said to me. Where are you headed?"

"My first stop is Texas. Not sure where after that."

A young man just out of training. "I'll pray for your safety, Private. God go with you." She moved on down the line, filling drinks and playfully changing the subject when overeager men stepped over the line of propriety. No matter how tired she was at the end of the day, pleasure at being able to brighten even a few moments of time for these men refreshed her as much as she suspected it did for them.

Breakfast rush over, Betsy mingled among the few lasting customers, mainly folks from the surrounding area of Colorado Springs. Most complained of the unusually cold winter predicted and the hardships they'd have to endure caring for the livestock.

"Just got a telegram," Gloria said, stopping to stand beside Betsy. "Got another train arriving this evening with some wounded soldiers who have booked a couple of rooms. It seems they plan on staying for a while and base housing is full. Until we get some more girls hired, the hotel needs extra hands preparing the rooms. Do you mind?"

"No, I'm happy to help." Betsy set the pitcher of water on the lunch counter and headed for the stairs. Occasionally they had soldiers stay a night or two, and they certainly livened up the place. More than one Harvey Girl always seemed to quit soon after with a ring on her finger.

Betsy sighed. They already had too few hands for the work as it was. Well, she'd do the best she could to make their rooms welcoming. If only there were fresh flowers to be had.

After putting clean linens on the beds and making sure the furnishings were dust free, she set a pad of paper and fresh ink pens on each nightstand. The men might want to write a letter home to let their families know when they'd arrive. It might be a small gesture, but she knew they appreciated anything they received to make their stay more pleasant.

With one last glance around each room, she closed the doors. Her job was done.

Planting her hands on her lower back, she leaned to pop out the kinks. One more meal time and she could enjoy the softness of her bed. Tomorrow, she'd visit the prison camp and see where she was needed the most. Being a farm girl, she could even do light nursing if the need arose. A little blood never hurt anyone.

She headed back down the stairs as the train whistle blew again and got into her assigned spot to welcome home the heroes. The other girls also took up their positions, chattering excitedly, smiles in place. Betsy shook her head. Yes, one of them would fall in love within the next couple of days or she would eat her apron.

A wheelchair approached the hotel's double doors, and Betsy rushed to assist, blinking back tears at the sight of the man's pants pinned to above his knees. She pushed the door open as wide as possible and blinked away the signs of her pity. These proud soldiers wanted joy, not sorrow.

"A little to the right, old man, and we'll be inside." The soldier in the chair reached out a hand to keep from bumping into the wall. "Then turn left. There's an empty spot at a nearby table."

Gracious, thought Betsy. The man pushing the wheelchair was blind, his hat pulled low over his face. "Let me help you." She placed her hands over those of the man pushing the wheelchair.

"I've got it," he said sharply.

Betsy jerked. "Spencer?"

4

Tears pricked Betsy's eyes. Spencer had returned blind, his beautiful blue eyes covered by dark glasses. Her hand covered her mouth.

"A smidge to the left, Spencer, and he'll be situated. There is an empty chair to the right of your friend."

"I won't be eating in the dining room. Please have someone escort me to my room and have a meal sent up." He removed his hat and held himself rigid, his face straight ahead.

"I'll escort you." Betsy crooked her arm. "Take my arm."

"I would prefer someone else."

Her heart sank. He might as well have punched her, so painful were his words. Their friendship seemed to have disappeared along with his sight. What had she done to offend him? "But—"

"Please, Betsy, honor my wish in this." His cold tone sent a rivulet of ice down her spine.

"Very well." She lowered her arm and stepped back.

"I'll return with someone more preferable to your taste." She rushed into the kitchen and leaned against the door, closing her eyes. Again, she'd allowed herself to feel something for a military man only to have those desires squelched.

"What's wrong?" Gloria's dark eyes peered at her over a load of freshly washed towels.

"The young man I've been writing to these last four months has returned." Betsy swiped the back of her hand across her eyes, thankful the Harvey Company did not allow the waitresses to wear makeup. If they did, she'd resemble a raccoon.

"That's wonderful, isn't it?"

"It should be." A sob lodged in her throat. "Instead, he's returned without his sight and wants nothing more to do with me, while I would like nothing more than to be of service to him."

Gloria set the towels on the counter and opened her arms. Betsy stepped into her warm embrace and allowed herself, if only for a moment, to pretend it was her mother who comforted her. "He doesn't want me anywhere near him."

"Of course he doesn't, you dear girl." Gloria set her at arm's length. "He thinks of himself as less than a whole man and can't bear for you to view him the same way."

"I would never think of him that way." The idea was ludicrous. Didn't Spencer know from her letters the type of woman she was? She covered her face with her hands. Had it all been nothing more than a way to fill his time while he was overseas? If he could believe her capable of such cold unfeeling, he wasn't the man she thought he was. Still, she'd grown to care for him, very much. "He wants someone to escort him to his room and bring up dinner, and he doesn't want that someone to be me."

"I'll take care of it. You take a few minutes to regain control of your emotions before returning to work.

There are plenty of other wounded soldiers that could use your help." Gloria hurried to the dining room.

Betsy had one last thing to do in regards to Spencer. She dashed upstairs to her room and pulled the latest letter she'd written to him from her drawer. She spritzed the rose-colored stationary with her toilet water and slid it into an envelope. The scented pages told him of her true feelings for him, and how they'd grown over the last few months. He may never read it, may never know it is in his room, but she wanted to leave it anyway. It would be her last letter to him.

She made her way to his room and placed the envelope on top of the polished dresser. Her heart ached to know he might never read the declaration of her feelings. She whirled as the sound of approaching footsteps sent her scurrying back into the hall. She ducked around the corner before she was spotted.

Gloria escorted Spencer, leaving him at the open door to his room. "I'll leave you to acquaint yourself with your surroundings," she told him. "Dinner will arrive in a few minutes."

"Thank you." Spencer entered his room, one hand outstretched, then slammed the door.

"I see you peeking," Gloria set her hands on her rounded hips.

Betsy's face flamed. "I only wanted to see that he made it safely." She stepped out and joined the head waitress.

"That's why I escorted him myself. I'll have one of the kitchen aides deliver his food. The two of us need to get back to the dining room."

Betsy nodded and hurried back to work. The moment she stepped back into the dining room, her gaze fell on the man in the wheelchair that Spencer had arrived with. She rushed to his side. "May I get you a refill on your coffee?"

"I would love one." He smiled up at her. "I'm Private Ralph Benson. Don't mind the good doctor. He's a bit surly, but you'll grow to like him in time."

"I knew him from…before." Betsy grabbed the carafe of coffee from the center of the table and refilled his mug. "I thought we were close friends. How did it happen, his…blindness?"

"A German soldier, impersonating one of our men, was brought into the medical tent. When the doctor discovered the man's true identity there was a scuffle. Dr. Gregory suffered a cut down his side and a head injury." Ralph shrugged. "It's a crying shame. He was a great doctor."

"Is his injury permanent?" Tears filled her eyes.

"No one knows for sure. A blow to the head can be tricky. Now, me," he patted his leg. "I stepped on a landmine. A doctor cut off what was damaged and stitched me up. I'm the lucky one, I guess. I'm an accountant by trade. I can still do that from a wheelchair. But a doctor needs his eyes, you know?"

"You are a very brave man, Private Ralph Benson. I will pray that God blesses you in your future." Betsy laid a hand on his shoulder. She'd also pray that God would lessen the pain in Spencer's heart. "You have been given a room on the ground floor. Let me know when you're ready to retire, and I'll wheel you back."

"Beautiful and generous." Ralph grinned. "I'm blessed indeed if your face is the last one I see before falling asleep."

"You, sir, are a flatterer." She blew him a kiss on her way to the next table. If only for a moment, the private had lifted her spirits and made the last two hours of her job pass a bit more pleasantly.

*

Spencer felt along the wall until he came to the window. He fought the latch until it popped free. With Betsy's scent tormenting him, he craved fresh air no matter how cold. He'd known she was still at the El Otero Hotel the moment he'd stepped into the front doors. The sweet scent of her letters followed him everywhere, even into his rented room.

Within minutes the frigid air forced him to close the window. He shivered and located his duffel bag. He could at least unpack his things while waiting for his meal. The closer he got to the dresser, the stronger the smell of Betsy's toilet water.

He ran his hand along the top of the dresser. There. So, she had left him a letter. He almost tossed it, but instead, decided to leave it. He had kept every one of her letters, why stop now? He removed the stack of envelopes tied with brown string from his bag and placed it in the drawer before covering them with his socks.

Once he'd finished unpacking his few items, placing his beloved harmonica beside his lamp, he sat on the edge of the bed. Maybe he should have someone read Betsy's letter to him, but he wasn't ready to admit that he might never be able to read for himself again. No, he'd wait until he'd lost all hope.

If he had his sight, he could stare at the wall. As it was, he saw nothing but the outline of the glowing lampshade. He could turn off the light, but then he'd have nothing but darkness.

The entire flight from France he'd listened to the happy conversations of soldiers returning home to their gals. But the closer Spencer drew to home, the more bitterness ate at him. He couldn't burden a woman with an invalid. Now he was resigned to a life of having his mother do everything for him.

His parents' farm was a short train ride north. He could head out tomorrow. He was a doctor. He didn't need anyone else to tell him only time would tell whether his sight would return. The lovely Betsy could find someone new. And she would—there were plenty of fine fellows to choose from. Men who were whole in body and mind.

"Good evening, sir." A woman called from the open door. "I've brought your dinner." The tray clattered as she set it on a table. "If you walk to the right of the bed, you'll find a small table with two chairs. Would you like me to wait until you've finished?"

"Absolutely not." He couldn't abide the thought of being watched like a sideshow freak while he ate. "I'll set the tray outside the door when I've finished."

"Oh, but I thought—"

"I'm very aware of what you thought." Keeping the bed to his left, he made his way to the table.

"It's a mite cold in here. Would you like an extra blanket?"

"No, thank you. I'll be fine." He fumbled around until he managed to pull out his chair and sit down. "You may leave me now and close the door, please." He waited for the click of the door before feeling for his eating utensils.

Maybe he should have had her stay. He had no idea what food was on his plate or where the items were situated in regards to the hands of a clock. He groaned and stuck his finger into what felt like mashed potatoes. Near that was a round bread roll. He lifted the plate to his nose and turned it, sniffing in the aroma of roast beef. He poked around until he found what he thought might be green beans next to the meat. With his hands as messy as a toddler's, he was ready to eat.

He ate, grateful for the solitude. When finished, he wiped his hands on his napkin, gathered everything onto the tray, and then stood. He picked up the tray, shuffled his way to the door, and froze. If he didn't know exactly where the doorknob was, how could he hold the tray and open the door?

Footsteps passing by alerted him to the fact he wasn't alone. "Hello? I could use some help."

The door opened and the soft scent of rose water washed over him. Of course it would have to be Betsy who came to his aid. She was probably doing the last of her evening chores. "Spencer, what's wrong?"

He thrust the tray forward. "My hands were full. I

couldn't open the door." Once she took the tray, he slammed the door closed.

The soft clearing of her throat told him she was still in the room. She coughed to cover the sound of her laugh. "It isn't really proper for me to be alone in your room with you, Spencer. I'll leave now." She chuckled and opened the door. A second later it closed and Spencer collapsed on his bed in shame. He allowed himself a few moments of self-pity before getting back to his feet.

He'd not be the brunt of a joke again. He'd spend the evening memorizing every inch of his room so that breakfast would go much smoother.

By the time he finished, his shins would no doubt sport bruises come morning, but he could count the steps to every stick of furniture and the door. Even without the lamp to guide him, he could traverse his room without fail. With a sense of accomplishment, he shed his uniform, donned his nightclothes, and then slid under the covers.

Outside his door, a couple conversed, the woman's giggles shrill. Spencer slapped his pillow over his ears. Would every moment bring him a reminder that he was alone?

Of course, his mother would say a man was never alone, not with God at their side. Where was God when Spencer hit his head? Why was his reward for trying to stop another soldier from being shot losing his own sight? No, Spencer had a bone to pick with God and intended to pray about it someday. Today was not that day.

He fell asleep with the memory of the single kiss he'd shared with Betsy on his mind.

5

"You're lucky, Betsy." Gloria handed her some rolled bandages. "There are only two ways into Camp Carson, by train and automobile. If you had need to go farther, you'd have to fly. The passage north is blocked by snow. The older folks are saying it won't clear until spring. I suppose some folks could get through on horseback and on foot, but few will try."

Betsy shook her head. "I've no need to go farther than the camp." She added the bandages to the basket on her arm. Inside was a Bible, a letter of recommendation from Gloria, and a pack of stationary. She needed to hurry to catch the train headed for the camp. Once there, she was informed she would catch a ride with the soldiers on a military vehicle.

With a deep breath and a tight hold on her basket, she marched through the dining room and onto the street. Several of the soldiers she'd served breakfast to waited for her on the sidewalk.

One tipped his hat and offered his arm. "We couldn't let you travel to the camp alone, miss."

"Thank you." The five men treated her like a princess as they helped her on the train and got her situated. They gave her a bench to herself, but positioned themselves all around her to discourage other passengers from entering into conversation with her.

"Have you ever been to the camp?" A freckle-faced young man, who looked still wet behind the ears, leaned across the seat.

"No, I haven't. I'm going to see whether I can be of some service in the hospital. Maybe read from the Bible or write letters back home for the wounded." She set the basket next to her and smoothed her skirt tight around her.

"Are you going to help those Germans?" The private curled his lip.

"If need be." Betsy met his gaze. "All men are created equal in the eyes of God, don't you believe?" She'd been warned that some would not look kindly to her willingness to help prisoners as well as wounded American soldiers, but her heart urged her forward. She'd made the decision when Spencer was overseas, and she found no reason to change her mind now that he had returned. What if he had been taken prisoner, or one of these other young soldiers? She hoped that somewhere in Germany a kind woman was giving America's soldiers a bit of comfort.

"One of them could have been the one who caused your beau to lose his eyesight."

Betsy closed her eyes and tightened her hands in her lap. "He isn't my beau. Dr. Gregory was nothing more than a pen pal." How her heart ached at the lie. She might not have been more than that to Spencer, but he had become much more to her. How foolish of her to cross the line between friendship and caring. Hadn't she learned her lesson with Lloyd?

"Yes, private, one of them could be the responsible

person, but that doesn't make him any less than God's creation. The man was fighting for his beliefs, misguided though they might be, the same as you."

"Well, I'm glad my girl doesn't have such foolish ideas about helping the enemy." The young man plopped back in his seat. While the other soldiers remained courteous and stayed where they were, they avoided Betsy's eyes.

She sighed. "Don't you gentlemen see? What if you were a prisoner in a foreign country? Wouldn't you want a woman to ease your pain a bit even if she didn't agree with your ideas of right and wrong? These prisoners will be here until this war is over. Who knows how long that will be."

"Ma'am, these Nazis are killing innocent people."

"Should we do the same? These men are following orders, same as you." She lifted her chin. "I don't condone their behavior, but they are still God's children."

"Leave her alone, Gilbert." An older man, a sergeant if Betsy read his stripes correctly, waved a hand. "You know she's right. Put your Irish dander back where it belongs and be respectful." He winked. "Ma'am, he hasn't seen a lick of fighting yet. Camp Carson is his first station. Pay him no attention. I'm Sergeant Harris. Blessed to meet you."

"Likewise." Betsy smiled. "I understand his enthusiasm. I wish I could have joined up myself, but became a Harvey waitress instead."

"You're still serving your country, without a doubt." He stood and held out a hand to help her to her feet as the train screeched to a halt. "I'll escort you to the infirmary. Some of these enlisted men can be quite the scoundrels when a pretty woman is in the vicinity."

"Thank you." Oh, how she wished it was Spencer escorting her. Still, if he wanted nothing to do with her, the sergeant made a very pleasant substitute. Why couldn't she find a nice man who wasn't in the military?

Sergeant Harris helped her into a jeep that would take them from the train to the camp. Betsy settled in and gazed wide-eyed out the window. She couldn't help but feel as if she were embarking on a new adventure. The interesting experiences had never stopped from the moment she signed her Harvey contract. With two months left, she needed to decide whether she planned to renew or not.

The rumbling automobile they rode in passed through a gate with a sign welcoming them to Camp Carson. A twelve-foot fence, rimmed with barbed wire, enclosed the compound.

"There's the infirmary, Miss Colter. There are two wings—one for the prisoners and one for the American soldiers. I'm sure they will have more than enough work for you to do."

"I'm looking forward to it."

The jeep stopped in front of a concrete block building with 34th General Hospital painted over the door. "Thank you, Sergeant Harris. I can find my way from here." Betsy thrust out her gloved hand.

The sergeant gave it a firm shake. "May I escort you on your next visit?"

She bit her bottom lip, then nodded. "Next Sunday, after church. I plan on making this a weekly excursion."

"Next Sunday will be the highlight of my week. I'll be living on base, but will be there to greet you at the station for sure."

Betsy sighed and opened the hospital door. It did no good to dream that Spencer was the one escorting her, although that was her heart's desire.

A doctor in a white coat greeted her as she approached a desk. "I'm Dr. Cleary, may I help you?"

"I've come to volunteer my services. I can do light nursing, read or write letters. Wherever I am needed." She pulled a letter of recommendation from Gloria out of her basket. "I work at the El Otero."

"I don't care where you work, my dear, we're glad to have you. I've some forms for you to fill out." He handed her a clipboard with several sheets of paper hanging from it. "Fill these out, check where you would most like to donate your time, and the day you're available. Then, return next week. I'll have to have someone verify you're an American citizen before you can actually do any volunteering."

Disappointed, she nodded. "I understand." She expelled a deep breath and took a seat in a straight back chair against the wall. She might as well take her time. The train returning to Colorado Springs didn't arrive for three hours.

She had just signed her name to the last sheet and approached the desk when the hospital doors opened. In walked Spencer, pushing Ralph's wheelchair. Betsy held a finger to her lips to signal for Ralph to keep quiet that she was there. As softly as possible, she skirted past them and headed for the safety of the door.

"I know you're there, Betsy." Spencer's deep voice rolled over her like thunder on a summer day. "Are you ill?"

Was he worried? "No, I'm filling out volunteer paperwork."

"Why?" His brow furrowed. "Aren't you busy enough?"

"My reasons are my own." How dare he question her?

"Pardon me. You're right. I'm butting in where I don't belong. Ralph, ring for the doctor."

Ralph reached forward and pressed a bell on the desk. "I guess we'll see you on the return train, Miss Colter. We were able to hitch a ride with a field worker on the way here, but will have to ride the train back. Save us a seat." He flashed her a grin.

She laughed. "One seat or two?"

*

Spencer stiffened at her implied jab. Of course she

would wonder. He'd been a bear to her. "Two, please." His shoulders slumped. It wasn't Betsy's fault that he was now blind. He shouldn't take out his feelings on her.

Heavier footsteps headed their way and Betsy excused herself. Ralph greeted the doctor who walked them down the hall and into one of the examining rooms. "It's good to see the two of you fellas working together."

"Yes, sir. Together, we make a whole." Spencer slid his foot out to the side until he located a chair.

"So, it's like that, is it? Feeling rather sorry for yourself despite the fact you're still breathing?" The doctor shuffled some papers. "I have your charts here. Private Benson, you're scheduled to return home in a week."

"Yes, sir, but the pass is blocked."

"That isn't a problem. We can fly both of you home if you'd like. But Dr. Gregory, I recommend you stay. We may be able to fly you home, but medical care will have to wait until spring unless you have a family doctor at home. Would you be staying on base?"

"No, sir. I'm on medical leave and prefer to stay at the hotel. I was told base housing was full, and the hotel is more comfortable." This way he wouldn't be a burden to his mother.

"Well, we'll see if we can't get you back to active duty. If your sight returns, that is. Otherwise, once I determine we've done all we can, you'll receive a medical discharge. It's perfect that you're staying at the hotel. We just had one of their girls volunteer here. I'll ask her to help you in any way she can. She'll return each Sunday and can escort you once Benson here leaves."

An icy hand gripped his heart. Betsy would be his caretaker? "What about her job?"

"No worries, there." The doctor grinned. "The head waitress is an old friend of mine. She'll work it out so

Betsy can accommodate both you and her job."

Great. Spencer rested his chin in his hand. His heart would never survive daily time spent with the beautiful Betsy. His resolve to keep his distance emotionally would crumble. Still, the thought of her waiting hand and foot on him as if he were an infant rankled. "Isn't there someone else we can get? Maybe I could hire someone."

"Do you have a problem with Miss Colter? She seemed like a fine, caring woman." The doctor's voice sounded worried. "Do you have an unlimited amount of funds to hire a companion?"

"No, sir." Spencer straightened. "I'll be fine with Miss Colter."

Ralph laughed. "He exchanged letters with Miss Colter while overseas. I think it bothers him that he'll have to rely on her to take care of him. Me? I'd like nothing more than to have a beauty like her by my side every day, but I'll have to settle for one of my sisters for now."

With his congenial attitude, the private wouldn't stay single for long, no legs or not. There would be a bevy of beauties waiting to welcome him home. Spencer, on the other hand? Well, who wanted a man who walked into walls and stuck his hands in his food?

He made the decision to look on Betsy as nothing more than a nurse. If he did, maybe he could pull his heart away from the way her letters made him feel or the way his heart raced every time he caught a whiff of her delicate rose water or heard the slight huskiness of her voice.

"Private Benson, I'll send someone for your things and fly you home tomorrow," the doctor said. "Dr. Gregory, I will see you on Sunday. Try to have a better attitude, all right? A good attitude is part of the healing process."

Spencer stood. "How do you propose I find my way back to the hotel? Do you have a white cane or a seeing eye dog?" He cringed at the spiteful tone to his voice.

"I'm sure Miss Colter, having nowhere else to go until the train arrives, is still in the waiting room. I'll fetch her for you." The sound of the doctor's marching footsteps echoed down the tiled hall.

"You've got it bad, mate." Ralph bumped his leg with the chair.

"What do you mean?"

"Your reluctance to have Miss Colter nurse you only shows how much you really care for her."

"Don't be ridiculous." Betsy could never find out his true feelings. Her pity would be his undoing.

"Here we are." The doctor didn't have to say anything. Spencer knew Betsy had arrived by the sound of her soft footsteps. "Miss Colter has agreed to be your companion at any time she is available."

Spencer scowled.

"Don't look so happy, Spencer. You've just increased my work load." Betsy tapped his arm. "It's time to make our way to the train. Private Benson, it was a pleasure meeting you. God go with you." With those words, she led Spencer rather forcibly from the room, not slowing her pace until they stepped outside.

"There are some rules to go along with our arrangement." She slipped her arm from his. "One, you will remove the scowl from your face every time I walk into the room. Two, I have a job. If you summon me and I don't arrive immediately, I insist you be patient. While you will be a priority, my employment with the Harvey Company is number one. You will have to learn to do many things yourself. I will help you learn. Any questions?"

For once, he was speechless. He would never have thought that sweet, mild-mannered Betsy had a drill-sergeant side. He rather liked her with her temper up.

"Well? Cat got your tongue? You've never been at a loss for words before."

He fought to keep a grin from spreading. "You've

been perfectly clear. I will do my best to abide by your rules."

"Good." Betsy slipped her arm back through his. "We'll have to pick up the pace. The train is coming. I will guide you. One foot in front of the other."

She set off at a pace fast enough to keep Spencer in fear of his life. When he needed to step up, she told him, if something was in his path, she veered him in another direction, until before he knew it, they were on the train platform.

"There are three steps up to the train car." She took his hand, taking his breath away, and placed it on a metal railing. "Use that as a guide. Once you are up, turn left."

He did as she instructed, almost bolting down the aisle when she placed her hands on his hips. "Please forgive my forwardness, but you can easily trip going down the aisle, since it is narrow."

She steered him to his seat, settled him in and left him wondering what in the world he was thinking to agree to let Betsy be his guide. His sides still tingled from her touch. He was a goner for sure.

6

Betsy settled onto the seat next to Spencer and flipped through the pages containing information about the types of duties she'd be called upon to do during her volunteer hours. She tried to focus on the words in front of her, but her traitorous emotions insisted on dwelling on how wonderfully strong Spencer felt under her hands as she guided him. She would have to find another way to lead him that didn't involve touching.

"What are you reading?" Spencer turned his face toward her.

"My volunteer obligations."

"What does it say?"

So he wanted conversation. Fine. She folded the papers and put them in her purse. She had agreed to help Spencer in any way she could. Keeping him entertained in his dark world most likely fell under helping him. "Basically, I'm there to read to them, fluff pillows, write letters and keep the men company. Anything that brings them a small amount of comfort."

"You're a regular angel of mercy, aren't you?" His lip curled.

"I'd like to think I'm doing what God has called me to do." She clenched her hands to keep from swatting him. "Look, *Dr.* Gregory, I'm sorry you were wounded, but that was not my fault and I will not stand by and allow you to steal my joy."

"Joy? Hearing from God?" He shook his head. "You go back to your simple pleasures, and I'll stare out the window at nothing."

"You're being a boor."

"I suppose I am. My apologies."

"I'm here to listen, Spencer, if you want to talk about how you're feeling." She leaned forward to peer into his face, wishing he'd remove the dark glasses so she could stare into his lovely eyes.

"There's nothing to say."

He didn't need to say anything. His wounded pride and shattered heart were loud and clear. Tears stung Betsy's eyes. He might not be the same carefree, fun-loving soldier who had left for Germany months ago, but he was still her Spencer.

They spent the rest of the ride in silence. When the train screeched to a halt in Colorado Springs, Betsy stood and placed a hand on Spencer's arm. His muscles rippled under her touch. No, she needed to steel herself against his attractiveness. She was nothing more than a nursemaid to him. It would be best for her to remember that.

It would also be best if he laid a hand on her shoulder. That should be safe enough. She set his left hand on her right shoulder. Her skin burned under his touch, and she sighed. There was no safe way to guide him. "I'll go slow, Spencer. Pay attention to my movements."

He chuckled. "Your movements are a distraction, Betsy."

Gracious! Her face flamed. The man switched from sour to flirtatious faster than a hummingbird's wings. "Step down, then twice more." Once down the steps and safely on the platform, Betsy called out to a passing motorist.

"I'm capable of walking," Spencer said.

"I'm sure you are, but it looks like rain, and I don't relish getting soaked. It's much too cold and too close to Thanksgiving to chance taking ill." She stood back while the driver opened the door then watched as the kind older man helped Spencer inside. Betsy smiled her thanks and slid in beside Spencer.

"I'd forgotten how close we are to the holidays," Spencer said. "I need to send a telegram to my family. Will you summon someone to do it for me?"

"I'd be delighted. First thing tomorrow I'll have the front desk clerk take care of the telegram."

"Thank you." He sat back as the car merged onto the street.

If Spencer had family close by, why wasn't he preparing to go home? She bit back the urge to ask.

Back at the hotel, Betsy escorted Spencer to his room with the promise of sending up his dinner. The moment she stepped inside her own room, her gaze fell on his framed photograph. With a sigh that came from deep within, she laid the frame flat, not quite ready to put it away but not desiring to look upon it each time she walked into the room either.

She perched on the side of her bed and covered her face with her hands. What was she going to do about her feelings for him? Oh, why had she agreed to help him? Keeping her distance would have been the best, and safest, way to deal with him. Now she'd spend the majority of every Sunday in his company, her only respite her time at the hospital.

What about Sergeant Harris? She'd agreed to let him escort her next week. Surely, he would have a soft spot in his heart for a wounded soldier and not take offense that Spencer would need to travel to Camp Carson with them.

A glance at the gold watch on her wrist alerted her to the fact it was dinner time. She hurried to Spencer's door and knocked. "It's time for dinner."

After several minutes, he opened the door. "I asked to have it sent to my room."

"I think it will be better for you to learn to eat in public." She cocked her head and grinned. "It's extra work to bring your meal up. You want to learn to be self-sufficient, don't you?"

"Yes, but I'm not ready yet."

"Trust me, Spencer." She placed his hand on her shoulder.

"You must be the most stubborn woman on this planet." He stepped out and closed the door. "Don't blame me if you find yourself embarrassed by my poor table manners."

"I don't embarrass easily." She led the way down the stairs and into the dining room, where she requested a small table in the corner away from the longer ones used to serve the military diners. After making sure

Spencer was seated, she sat across from him and spread her napkin in her lap. "Your water goblet is to your left about six inches from your hand. Your wrapped silverware is below that."

She picked up her menu. "The recommended meal is braised chicken with asparagus. Is that sufficient or would you like me to read the rest of the menu?"

"That will be fine." He sat as rigid as a railroad tie, his eyes flicking to the menu in front of him. A nerve ticked in his right jaw.

"You will find this difficult at first, but it will become easier." Betsy reached across the table and patted his hand. "I can't be with you every minute. It's back to work for me tomorrow." She gave their order to their waitress.

"Dr. Cleary said arrangements had been made with the head waitress."

"Yes, for when you are in the dining room where I am working. You'll have to learn to get from your room down here on your own."

His face paled. "I'll stay in my room."

"Well, that will be a sad state to be in all the time." Betsy removed her hand. "You still have a lot of living to do."

He shrugged. "Maybe."

"Of course you do. What does the doctor think about your sight? Will it return?"

"Possibly. No one knows for sure." He fiddled with his fork. "In case it doesn't, I must resign myself to the fact I could be condemned to seeing only shadows for the rest of my life."

"You see shadows? That's great." Betsy clapped. "You'll get used to getting around on your own in no time, especially with the shiny cane he gave you."

"It's easy to be optimistic when you're whole." He snapped his napkin and spread it across his lap. "Our dinner is arriving."

"How did you know?" How could she convince him that he was as whole and capable as he'd always been? Spencer's life wasn't over, just changed. There was still so much he could do to contribute to society.

"I could smell the chicken, and I recognized our waitress's footsteps."

"See how well you're doing?" Betsy laughed. "You need to stop being a baby."

*

"You are a cruel woman." But maybe she was right. Spencer needed to stop feeling sorry for himself, especially since he'd caught a glimpse of the black type against the white of the hotel menu. A tiny seed of hope sprouted. He needed to stop being angry at God and, instead, trust that God knew what He was doing.

He squinted across the table, trying to make out Betsy's features. It was no use. He only saw what he remembered from their tender goodbye four months ago. Even the menu type was only a memory now.

"The chicken is at five o'clock on your plate. The asparagus is at nine and the rice at one. There is a roll balanced on the edge at eleven." Betsy placed his fork in his right hand. "With your left hand to guide you, you should be able to eat sufficiently."

Easy for her to say. He hated to get his hands dirty with food and there was no help for it when he couldn't see where to put his fork. "How do you expect me to cut my chicken into small enough pieces that I don't choke?"

"Oh. I hadn't thought of that. Let me cut your meat for you." She got up and moved to his side, filling his senses with her proximity. The woman was pure torture. In her desire to help him, she'd overstepped boundaries she wouldn't cross if he were a seeing man.

When she returned to her seat, and he could breathe again, Spencer concentrated on stabbing something on his plate each time the fork met the china. If he took his time and kept Betsy involved in conversation, maybe he wouldn't make too big of a fool of himself.

"Will you miss Ralph?" Betsy asked.

"Who?" Spencer paused, his fork half way to his mouth. It didn't take long for the food to fall off. He hoped it hadn't landed in his lap.

"The young man who lost his legs."

"I suppose. Benson was a jolly chap." Spencer tried to nonchalantly find the fallen food by rubbing his hand across the tablecloth. "It's good that he's going home."

"The asparagus has fallen back to your plate." She giggled. "It's dead center. Forgive me for laughing, but you're so serious in trying to hide your, uh, accident. Relax, Spencer, no one is paying us any mind, and I don't care if you've food smeared across your face."

"I've food on my face?" He dabbed all over with the napkin.

She laughed again. "No, I said I wouldn't care if you did. Enjoy your dinner. It's actually quite good."

He didn't understand the woman, not one bit. He stabbed something else with his fork. On one hand, she was caring and unselfish. On the other hand, she laughed at his discomfort and disability. He knew there was no malice in her teasing, but it still rankled. How could she make jokes when life had dealt him such a malicious blow? By the time they'd completed their meal, his neck and shoulders were strung as tight as a clothesline.

"Are you ready to go to your room or would you like to take a walk around the hotel grounds?" Betsy moved to his side. "The night is chilly, but clear. Fresh air might do us both some good."

"I'd prefer to head to my room." He stood and waited while she put his hand on her shoulder.

"Okay. I should be safe walking alone."

The little minx. He sighed. "I'll escort you." Once they stepped into the night air, he asked, "Are you afraid of being alone with so many military men around?"

"Oh, no." She stepped away from his hand and hooked her arm in his. "The men have never behaved like anything other than gentlemen."

"So, you tricked me."

"I suppose you could say that. It isn't good for you to spend so much time alone, Spencer."

"I'm perfectly capable of being in charge of my own life. You're my volunteer guide and helper, nothing more." While he had once enjoyed walking out with a pretty young woman, those days were over.

"I have no idea why I care whether you stay in your room and rot." She yanked free. If he wasn't mistaken, he clearly heard the sound of her foot stomping the brick walkway. "And furthermore, Dr. Gregory, I'd like to know where the happy soldier went."

Uh-oh, she'd called him by his surname again. "What do you mean?"

"You left here full of excitement and returned a bitter man who is drowning in a lake of self-pity."

"I lost my sight, and with it my youthful foolishness of thinking I could save the world."

"You didn't lose your life, Spencer, and you should stop acting as if you did. Put your hand on my shoulder. I'm ready to go back."

"I'm sorry. Let's continue the walk. You can describe to me what you see. Be my eyes."

She kept quiet for so long, he thought she would still insist on returning to their rooms. "Okay, but no further spiteful words or I promise I will leave you out here alone."

What a gutsy little thing. Maybe he'd nourish his sour attitude just to get her dander up. "I'll behave." It was time to stop fretting about his sight. Either it would be restored or he would learn to cope.

If God chose not to restore it, then Spencer would hire a companion to escort him when he left his parents' farm. But if, by some miracle, he regained his sight, he would kiss this beautiful girl again until she swooned, because it was her insistence and patience that kept him moving forward.

"Spencer, are you listening?"

"What? I'm sorry."

"I was describing the lovely ornate cement fountain in the shape of a lovely maiden pouring out an urn. Around the fountain are evergreen shrubs, juniper, I think, it's hard to tell in the dark."

"Sounds beautiful."

"But not as gorgeous as the night sky. Have you ever gazed upon a sky that appeared to be black velvet with diamonds scattered upon it? There's no moon and the view is breathtaking."

"I can see it in my mind." His leg brushed against a

bench, and he pulled her down to sit beside him. "Tell me more."

"The trees have lost their autumn vibrancy and reach toward the sky with skeletal fingers." She shuddered. "Occasionally, the branches rub together like dry bones."

"I can hear them." He removed his jacket and placed it around her shoulders. His hand brushed her cheek. The sky may look like velvet, but her skin was as soft. He wanted to take the liberty of putting his arm around her shoulders and pulling her close, to sit with her as they had on the train the day she fell asleep. Those days were gone, never to be retrieved. All he could do was move forward and watch as an undamaged man someday claimed her. Girls like Betsy didn't remain single for long.

They sat outside for a while longer while Betsy described the winter garden and Spencer listened. She portrayed a vivid picture, and he hated for the time to end, but the night was growing colder. He stood and held out his hand.

The windows of the hotel glowed with an amber light. An *amber* light. Not the usual white against black he'd been seeing. He smiled. Betsy was right. He needed to stop fretting and let time heal him. "It's too cold out here for you. Let's go back."

"You should take your jacket."

"No, I'm fine." He crooked his arm. When she tucked her arm through his and pressed close, he was as warm as if he were covered by a thick blanket.

All too soon they were standing in front of his room and she had returned his jacket. "Thank you, Betsy. I had a great time."

"You're welcome. I'll fetch you for breakfast sometime around seven."

Spencer stepped into his room and closed the door, then lifted his jacket to his nose and breathed in her sweet scent. He hung his coat on the bedpost and made his way to the dresser where her letter sat. Someday, he hoped to ask her to read it to him. He couldn't ask anyone else. Their words were private, meant only for the two of them even if they were only about day-to-day events.

He got undressed, folding his uniform and placing it across the back of the chair. The shapes of the furniture seemed more defined, increasing his belief that healing was taking place. He couldn't wait to discuss it with Dr. Cleary on Sunday. His first instinct was to call for Betsy, but he decided against it. He'd wait until his sight was either fully restored or the healing had halted. Why build up either of their hopes?

Someday, he wished to look into her beautiful eyes again. Until that day came, he would remain silent and pray the headaches and bad attitude stayed away. If he continued to act like the boor Betsy thought he was, he'd drive her away for sure.

And that would shatter his heart into pieces that numbered the stars.

7

"I don't think that soldier of yours is as immune to your charms as you might think." Gloria met Betsy in the hall one Sunday morning as Betsy made her way toward the stairs.

"What do you mean?" Betsy tugged on her white gloves.

"He's been asking about how you spend your Sundays after you drop him off at the hospital."

"You didn't tell him they've assigned me to the German wing, did you?" While Sergeant Harris had been detained the past two Sundays, Spencer was all the escort Betsy actually needed in order not to be swarmed by eager enlisted men on the train, but she had yet to inform him that she was providing comfort to the enemy.

"Of course not, goose. It's best to leave you as a woman of mystery." Gloria frowned at a waitress who was running late. "I wish I had twenty workers as efficient as you, Betsy. I sorely miss you on Sundays."

"Even the Lord took a day of rest." Betsy smiled. "You're a stern task mistress. I'm grateful for my day of rest."

"Some rest. You come back each Sunday evening exhausted."

"I'm fine." Gloves on, Betsy headed toward Spencer's room, Gloria on her heels. The head waitress and Betsy had been fast friends since Betsy's first day on the job. Sometimes, it was difficult to balance the line between friend and employee. "This is the last Sunday before Thanksgiving. My heart aches for all the wounded, American and otherwise, who will spend the holidays in the hospital."

"What goodies do you have in your bag today?"

"My Bible, of course, and a copy of Robinson Crusoe. I also managed to get my hands on a small tin of Jordan almonds. They will be a special treat." With the government rationing, anything made with sugar was a rarity. "Do you know the prisoners are primarily responsible for cooking their own meals? The ones that are not in the infirmary, of course." She cut a sideways glance at Gloria. "They prefer potatoes over a lot of the other things and refuse to eat corn on the cob. They say they won't eat anything meant for cows and pigs." She giggled.

"You have an exciting life. Don't get me wrong, but with the war, there is no better time to be a Harvey Girl. We get to serve our men and our country good meals with a smile when so many women are building airplanes. Enough chatting or I'll be late." Gloria rushed downstairs.

Betsy knocked on Spencer's door. After several minutes, the door opened, and he stepped out. "Good morning," she said. "Did you sleep well?"

He nodded, his eyes twinkling. "I did."

"Do you need your glasses? The sun is quite bright today."

He patted his pocket. "I have them close, just in case."

She led him to the dining room, the routine so familiar, Spencer walked beside her as if he could see the way. Once seated, Betsy ordered toast and tea while Spencer ordered a full egg breakfast. She raised her eyebrows at his appetite, but held her tongue. If the man wanted to ride the train on a gorged stomach, who was she to say anything?

"Miss Colter?"

"Sergeant Harris." Betsy stood and held out her hand.

"I'm sorry I haven't kept my promise to escort you to the camp. I've been ill with the flu and unable to travel. I thought I was gonna croak there for a while, but I pulled through."

"I'm so sorry. If I'd known, I would have kept you company on my visits." She waved to an empty chair at a nearby table. "This is Dr. Spencer Gregory. I am his eyes to and from the hospital on Sundays. Won't you join us for breakfast?"

"Sure, we've got time before the train arrives. It's a pleasure to meet you, Doctor." Sergeant Harris pulled up a chair.

"Likewise." Spencer thrust out his hand, high spots of color on his cheeks. The familiar tic in his jaw that alerted her to the fact he was annoyed made its appearance. "If you've somewhere to be, Betsy is perfectly safe with me by her side."

"Oh, no. I've been looking forward to this for weeks. I feel like I've been knocked out for way too long." Sergeant Harris scanned the menu. "Pancakes, please," he told the waitress.

Betsy followed the back-and-forth banter until she thought her head would fall off. If she didn't know any better, she'd think Spencer was jealous. Good. It wouldn't hurt for him to know that other men desired her company.

After a breakfast of Sergeant Harris rambling like a parrot and Spencer keeping his features locked in ice, Betsy wanted nothing more than to go to her room and hide from both of them. Instead, she grabbed her basket and waited for the weight of Spencer's hand on her shoulder. She could have sworn his eyes flicked to Sergeant Harris's for a second as a slow smile spread across his face. He would tell her if his sight was returning, wouldn't he?

She narrowed her eyes and studied his face. Like a child caught peeking, Spencer grabbed his glasses from his pocket and slid them on. Hmm, very interesting. His behavior warranted her paying a bit closer attention.

With a man on each arm, feeling like a carnival prize coveted by two ambitious young boys, Betsy was soon seated on the train with Sergeant Harris next to her and Spencer scowling from across the aisle. This type of behavior would never do. Although not a stranger to a man's attention, she'd never been in this type of situation before.

While her heart still yearned for the man in Spencer's letters, it was nice to feel the sergeant's admiration. She had yet to see the man's unpleasant side, where Spencer had shown he could be, well, snarky, for lack of a better word. She sighed and rested her head in her hand.

By the time they arrived at the hospital, her head pounded, and once again the two men tugged her along between them. "Stop it." She yanked free. "I can walk of my own accord, thank you. Sergeant, while I appreciate you following up on your word to provide me with an escort, it isn't needed. However, Spencer does need help, so I'm leaving you to lead him to his appointment. Now, when the two of you can once again behave like gentlemen, I'll be glad to spend time with either one, or both, of you." She marched away, head high.

*

She glanced over her shoulder. The startled looks on the men's faces left her with the giggles. Ignoring the curious glances of the nurses, Betsy headed toward the wing that housed the German wounded and one bed in particular, which held a young man missing an arm.

"How are you, Schmidt? Good? I've brought paper to write your letter home."

He grinned despite the pain shadowing his features. "I will have to spell each word for you, as my mother does not read English."

"That's fine. I'm here for two hours." Betsy took a seat in the chair beside his bed. "I've candied almonds. Would you like one?"

He sat up straighter and peeked into her bag. "Ya."

"When we finish, I will read the next chapter of our story." While she sat beside the young man's bed, she read loud enough for the others in the dormitory style room to hear. All of them may not understand the words, but the sound of her voice seemed to bring them comfort.

"It is good that you are a friend of Germany," Schmidt said. "But I fear your country will be…angry?"

"I'm not a friend of Hitler's beliefs." She paused her pen on her paper. "But I believe that all men are equal in the eyes of God and that He has called me to minister to all of them, not just Americans."

"This God you speak of. He also loves those who fight for Germany?"

Betsy took a deep breath. "Yes, he does, but that does not mean He approves of the senseless killing of innocent people. It only means that he loves each of the men in the army. Does this make sense to you?"

"This talk would get you killed in my country."

"Yes, I'm sure it would. Let's finish your letter, shall we?"

*

It took some convincing to get Harris to point him in the right direction and let Spencer make his own way to the large white building, but the man finally left him. The hospital was hard to miss, even to someone with limited sight.

Spencer chuckled at Betsy's sassiness. He so enjoyed getting her riled. But he had acted like a fool and needed to apologize. The shadows were taking a more distinct shape lately and that had enabled him to see that Harris couldn't take his eyes off Betsy. Who could blame the man? Betsy was a looker for sure, and not only on the outside. Her inner beauty shined forth like the brightest star. Still, seeing and hearing how the man responded to every word she spoke had galled Spencer.

"Dr. Gregory, where's your beautiful companion?"

Dr. Cleary stepped into the waiting room.

"Already away doing her business."

"Come on back. Can you make it on your own by now?"

If the doctor only knew. It was time to come clean. Spencer entered the office and closed the door before sitting in a chair across from the desk. "I have a confession to make."

"Your sight is returning." The doctor grinned.

"It appears so." Of course the man would suspect, he was in the medical field, after all. "When did you know?"

"A couple of weeks ago. I'm not sure you completely realized it then, but your eyes followed me when I walked across the room."

"The healing has happened so gradually, and isn't complete yet, so at times I forget exactly how much I actually can see."

"That's great. Since you're stuck here for the winter, I could use your help with the German prisoners."

Spencer frowned. "Why not our own wounded? I don't cotton to helping the ones who blinded me. Besides, my sight hasn't fully returned."

"Maybe not, but you can listen to their medical complaints and direct the nurses. I've too much on my plate and could use the help. Since your friend Betsy is helping—"

"What?" Spencer knew she volunteered but he had assumed it was with the Americans.

"She's more than eager to help where there's the greater need." Dr. Cleary leaned back in his chair. "I thought you might feel the same way. I could put in a formal request for your help but would rather you offered."

"You'll have to put in the request. I won't do it voluntarily." Spencer stood and stormed from the office. In the waiting room, he plopped into a chair and prepared himself to wait for an hour and a half until Betsy joined him.

Care for the German prisoners? The doctor was off his rocker. Sure, Spencer had taken an oath, but that was to help Americans and their allies, not the enemy. He'd help if ordered to, but not before, and he doubted the doctor would follow up on his threat, especially with Spencer on medical leave.

The up-and-down journey of traveling through his blindness left him with little compassion for those he held responsible. What if he found himself faced with the very man who had attacked him? What if that man was dying and, as a prisoner of war, needed medical attention? Spencer wasn't sure how he would respond.

His mother would tan his hide if she knew the range of emotions coursing through him. She'd always taught him to look at another human through the eyes of God's love. Until the war, Spencer had been able to. Now things weren't so easy. He missed Ma's words of wisdom. Maybe it was time to write her a letter. No, he couldn't see well enough yet, and that wasn't a letter he wanted someone to write for him, not to mention he had forgotten to send that infernal telegram weeks ago.

Nurses and other medical personnel shuffled by him as if he wasn't there, all in a hurry to get somewhere important, leaving Spencer to wallow in his indecision and wonder how much longer until Betsy left the enemy to tend to one of America's fallen.

A small niggling in his conscience warned him of his

dangerous way of thinking. Hadn't he said a few days ago he would no longer hold God responsible for his injury? Then why the sudden return of bitterness? Why turn his back on what God's Word taught about helping his fellow man?

Spencer had a lot to think about, but not then. Knowing Betsy sat beside a German, most likely wiping his sweaty brow, patting his hand, reading to him in her soft voice, it was all enough to give Spencer indigestion and a pounding headache. He laid his head back against the wall and closed his eyes.

"Hello?" A gentle hand shook him awake. "Spencer? Are you ready to go?"

He opened his eyes to Betsy leaning over him, her smooth face creased with concern. Thankfully, he wore his dark glasses and she couldn't tell his sight was returning. He didn't know why he wanted to keep it a secret from her. Maybe it was the fact she wasn't forthcoming about the people she ministered to each Sunday. "I'm ready. You caught me napping."

"We need to find something for you to do after your doctor visits." She started to slip her arm through his, but stopped.

"I apologize for my behavior earlier. I was acting like a child." He crooked his arm. "Please."

"As long as you promise not to let it happen again."

"I promise to do my best." He grinned.

She shrugged, then linked her arm with his. "I guess I will have to be satisfied with that. We'd best hurry. My duties today took longer than normal. I'd hate to miss the train and have to find someone to drive us all that way."

"Then let's make like crazy for that train. Lead on."

Betsy took off at a fast walk, directing where he needed to put his feet with each step. "Now tell me if we're going too fast. I don't want you to fall."

"I'm okay." He felt like a heel for deceiving her, but he feared that once she knew he could see well enough to get around, their time together would stop, and she'd move on to the next needy guy. He wasn't ready for that to happen.

Back on the train, Betsy called out greetings to soldiers returning to the hotel, then plopped onto her seat. "These poor men. With the passage blocked, they can't get home for the holidays."

"Some are only here on leave until they return to Europe." Spencer settled down beside her. "Others have nowhere else to go, and the hotel is a lot more comfortable than base housing."

"I'll speak to the hotel manager about making everyone's stay a little more cheerful."

"Seeing all the pretty dolls is cheer-making enough for most of them."

"I suppose. I hope some of the girls aren't foolish enough to ask the soldiersto make promises they won't keep. Most of these men probably have a girl in every state, writing him letters, waiting anxiously for his return."

"You sound as if you speak from experience." Spencer placed his arm along the back of the seat.

"I do." She stiffened. "I was engaged to an army man who returned with a new wife. That's when I signed on as a Harvey girl. I almost joined the service as a nurse, but while I can tolerate the sight of blood most of the time, it isn't my favorite thing. Anyway, that's all water under the bridge."

"Do you think that was my intention when I asked you to write?"

"I was beginning to when so much time passed after your last letter, but then you showed up at the hotel and..." She shrugged.

His pulse relaxed at hearing her answer. To hear her say that she lumped him in the same category as her ex-fiancé would have wounded him to the core. "Well, your fiancé was a fool."

"Thank you. That means a lot to me."

"I'm pretty sure Sergeant Harris would agree." Spencer crossed his arms.

"Stop frowning. He is nothing more than a friend, same as we are."

As time had passed, Spencer realized he still wanted to be more than friends with the gorgeous, strong-willed, compassionate Betsy Colter. He needed to find a way to let her know his feelings. Maybe he could write her a letter before he dug a hole so deep that he couldn't find his way out.

"Helping you has given me a new purpose," she said. "If I choose not to renew my Harvey contract after Christmas, I could easily find employment as a companion for the disabled."

She looked on him as disabled? He couldn't blame her. That's exactly how he used to view himself, but no more. He wanted Betsy to see him as a man, a whole man. It was time to come clean.

"Betsy, I—"

"Oh, Spencer, it's snowing again." She got to her feet and gently pushed him into the aisle. "Let's go out in it."

"Yes, but I—"

"Do be careful going down the steps in case they're slippery. I'm not strong enough to catch you."

"Okay, but—"

"Come on. We don't want to miss dinner." She grabbed his hand and tugged.

Spencer sighed. He'd have to live the lie a little longer.

8

Betsy stood at one end of the dining room and watched Spencer as he interacted with his fellow soldiers. Occasionally, a laugh erupted at something one of the other men said. The sound warmed Betsy's heart. How far he'd come in the time he'd been there. He still exhibited moments of self-pity and bitterness, but those were coming fewer and farther between.

Her heart rejoiced and mourned at the same time. Once the way through Rabbit Ears Pass was melted, he'd leave Colorado Springs—and her. But that was months away. Unless… Ralph had been flown home by the military. Could the same happen for Spencer?

"Why the long face?" Gloria handed her a water pitcher.

"He'll be leaving me soon."

"Honey, he's a soldier. They always leave." With those encouraging words, she left Betsy holding the pitcher.

Gloria was right. Had Betsy learned nothing from Lloyd? Spencer was only at the hotel because he had nowhere else to go. Betsy shoved aside her disappointment and started refilling water glasses.

"Look at this, Doc." A soldier thrust a newspaper toward Spencer. "We just bombed the dickens out of the German port of Wilhelmshaven. We used 539 planes. Those Germans don't stand a chance."

Spencer glanced over at the paper and appeared to read. His eyes seemed to follow the words before he lifted his gaze and met Betsy's. He shoved the paper aside. "I can't read it, soldier."

"Oh, that's right. Sorry." The soldier began reading the paper out loud.

If his eyesight was returning, why would Spencer want to hide something so wonderful from her? They were at least friends, and friends shared good news with each other. Her hand shook as she poured, dribbling some of the water onto the tablecloth. Maybe Spencer didn't consider her a close enough friend. Maybe she really was nothing more than a temporary nursemaid. A plaything. Someone to relieve the boredom and helplessness of his blindness.

Of course, Dr. Cleary had asked her to be exactly that, but she'd hoped, in the deepest places of her soul, that Spencer would regard her differently. What a fool she had been.

Her letter! If his sight was returning, he'd read her deepest feelings. With the way things were between them currently, she couldn't let that happen. She needed to get that letter back.

After breakfast, most of the soldiers returned to the

train, but the few who were staying at the hotel moved to the common parlor. Betsy wanted to follow them and see how Spencer reacted when something required him to see, as the newspaper had.

The rest of the day passed in long hours of routine. Betsy's mind raced with possible scenarios for stealing back her letter, thus resulting in her taking two wrong meal orders. Gloria commented several times that Betsy needed to either pay more attention or take a break.

She couldn't take a break. Then her mind would have nothing else to occupy it but the letter. She avoided Spencer as much as possible so he couldn't sense her preoccupation. She'd never been good at lying. He'd spot her standoffishness at once. She usually talked a mile a minute.

She had just finished putting a clean stack of tablecloths in the supply closet when she heard the telltale thump of Spencer's cane. She froze and prayed he wouldn't find her.

"Good evening, Betsy."

"How did you know it was me?" She whirled, slamming her spine into the shelves.

"I smelled you." He leaned against the doorjamb. "I'd know the scent of your rose water anywhere. You spritzed my letters with it. "

Heavens, she'd spritzed the last letter, too, and quite heavily. "May I help you?"

"Shouldn't you be off work by now?"

"Do you need help finding your room?" She turned back to the tablecloths, which were threatening to topple onto the floor.

"No."

"Then, what?" She glanced over her shoulder.

"I thought you might like to have an ice cream with me or something." He quirked his mouth. "I know its cold, but I don't want to head to my room, and I'm tired of hearing the same news stories with each new group of soldiers who go into the parlor."

"I could read to you from the Bible."

"No, thanks. I'm not quite ready to confront God yet."

"Have you read Robinson Crusoe? I could—"

"I don't want to be read to, Betsy." He turned. "Never mind. I'll see you tomorrow."

She listened as he made his way down the hall. She understood his loneliness. She should find Spencer and apologize and have ice cream with him.

Right after she stole back her letter. She stepped into the hall and glanced both ways. Which way had he gone? To his room or back to the parlor? It would look suspicious if she ran into him close to his room.

"Lilly." She stopped one of the hotel maids.

"Yes, ma'am." The petite brunette turned.

"Have you cleaned room 108 yet?"

"Yes, and turned down the bed. Why?"

Betsy sighed. "No reason." She couldn't very well tell the maid she left something in there. That would lead to a lot of speculation and questions she didn't have answers for. "Have a good night."

The girl looked at her, puzzled, then shrugged and continued on her way. She was probably used to strange questions. Betsy chewed her bottom lip and headed to stand outside Spencer's room.

She plastered her ear to the door. Did no sound mean he wasn't in or did it mean he held the world's fastest record for falling asleep?

A person should never make rash decisions while grieving. Spencer's rebuke of her attempts to help him when he'd first arrived at the hotel had led her to do something foolish. It was all his fault.

From the moment he kissed her before leaving for Germany, Betsy had lost her focus. She wanted to help people, have a calling, follow God's leading. She had definitely decided that a relationship with a man, especially one in the military, was not for her. So, what was the problem?

"Betsy?"

She closed her eyes and turned to face Spencer.

"Did you change your mind about the ice cream?"

"Yes." She released the breath she was holding. She opened her eyes and smiled.

"Great. I thought you'd given me the brush off." He offered her his arm. "How long were you knocking?"

"Oh, I just got here." She glanced toward the ceiling, giving God thanks she'd been spared the mortification of being caught snooping in his room.

"Did you know that ice cream is used to bolster morale among the military men?" Spencer explained. "There's actually quite a competition going on among the different branches of our armed forces. They're all trying to outdo each other in who can serve the most ice cream to its troops."

"Fascinating. It's a good thing the hotel has some, despite the sugar and dairy rationing for civilians." Why was he suddenly talking faster than a runaway train?

"It definitely helps to have soldiers staying here." They settled at their usual table in a corner of the dining room.

Betsy spread her napkin in her lap, then ran her hands over it and smoothed it again, then again. Taking a gal out for ice cream seemed suspiciously like a date. She studied Spencer's strong jaw, the soft look in his eyes, and wondered what he was thinking as he stared over her left shoulder. He'd been full of conversation on his way to the dining room, now he'd clammed up.

He took a deep breath. "I'd like you to send a telegram for me."

"Of course." This is why he acted so nervous? "Who would you like the telegram to go to?"

"My mother."

*

Spencer focused on the fuzzy features of Betsy's face. While he was seeing better, he still couldn't read a word. He needed to mention to his doctor that prescription glasses might help. He wanted to be a doctor again. With the war continuing, his services were needed to save lives. He couldn't let his parents wonder why he wasn't writing any longer. It was time to come clean with them and with Betsy. No more secrets.

"What would you like me to write?" Betsy pulled a pen and an empty envelope from her pocket.

"First, I have something I need to come clean with you about." He twirled his fork on the tablecloth. "I'm not sure you've noticed, but—"

"That your sight is returning? I've suspected. How much can you see?"

"More than shadows now. Colors, and the light doesn't give me blinding headaches anymore, but reading and writing are still impossible." He straightened his shoulders. "I'm beginning to have faith that my eyesight will fully return someday."

"And now that you feel as you will no longer be a burden on your parents for an indefinite amount of time, you're willing to let them know you're still alive and kicking." "And I should have contacted them before. I know how worried they must be. Since you're in the know about my circumstances, I thought you'd be the most trustworthy to write my telegram."

"Uh-huh." She drummed her fingers on the tabletop.

"Have I made you mad?" Spencer leaned closer. "If you don't want to, I can get one of the other gals to help with the telegram."

"No." She expelled a deep breath. "When was the last time you wrote to your parents? Months? Since the last time you wrote me?"

"Yes." He was a heel, a creep, and deserved whatever tongue-lashing Betsy felt ready to dish out.

"So, they are left not knowing whether you are dead or alive." She stood. "Spencer Gregory, I am ashamed of you. It was bad enough for you to leave me hanging during your time in the hospital, but I'm only a doll you asked to write to you. Your parents deserve more. I will see you at breakfast to write your telegram."

"Wait." He shoved to his feet, but she was gone.

She was right. He had been horribly unfair to his parents in keeping silent. They probably feared him dead. He reached out a hand and stopped one of the waitresses. "Miss, does the hotel have a phone?"

"Yes, sir. The front desk does. Would you like me to show you?"

"Please." He could call the general store a mile from his parents' farm and the proprietor could deliver a message. He'd put more information in the telegram tomorrow.

He followed the waitress to the front desk. "I'd like to make a call."

"Now?" The man said. "It's almost nine p.m."

"Oh." Another drawback of being blind. Spencer had no idea what time of the day it was. Self-pity, his new friend, threatened to rest once again on his shoulders. "Thank you. Instead, I find myself in need of an escort to my room."

"Very well, sir." Within seconds, Spencer once again followed the waitress.

She stopped outside his door. "Will there be anything else, sir?"

"No, thank you." He entered his room and removed his jacket. He ran his hand over the jacket. If his sight didn't improve soon, he'd have to hang up the khaki uniform for good. What if he could never practice medicine again? What would he do with his life? He reached for the newspaper beside his bed and strained to read even the bold print of the headline. It was no use. The words were nothing more than black smudges against the white.

He fell backward on the bed. The day after tomorrow was Thanksgiving, and he'd have to dig deep to find things to be thankful for. Betsy was one, even if she was angry with him. His life was another, even if he was blind. He supposed he had plenty to thank God for, and it was about time Spencer stopped blaming Him for the cruel twist life had taken and start making the best of things. If he didn't regain his full sight, he needed to ask God what path he should take in his uncertain future.

He got up and moved to the window and thrust it open. Cold air blasted his face along with the kisses of snowflakes. He closed his eyes and pictured the pure whiteness of snow in the moonlight, the tint of blue in the shadows. They'd probably have a white Christmas, and God willing, Spencer's sight would have fully returned by then. What a gift that would be.

Once he could see, he would tell Betsy how much she meant to him. He couldn't tell her now. Her sweet nature would compel her to accept him even damaged as he was. He wouldn't ask any woman, much less one like her, to tie themselves to him. Not until he was whole again.

If God decided not to restore his sight, maybe he'd ride the rails until he was too old. That life would be adventurous for a half-blind man. He chuckled at his childhood dream of being a hobo and closed the window.

He couldn't read Betsy's letter, but he could hold it, smell it, run his fingers over the writing. He went to his dresser and ran his hand across the smooth surface.

The letter was gone.

9

Betsy's letter to Spencer crackled in the pocket of her apron as she folded linens for the Thanksgiving dinner the next day. Had he noticed it gone? Had he known it was there in the first place? She hoped not. If so, who else would take it but her? She'd need to avoid him.

"Head's up," Gloria said as she sailed past, smoothing her brunette hair into place. "New manager just arrived. I've heard he's a beast."

A new manager right before the holidays? They'd been just fine with Gloria overseeing everyone. Betsy glanced at her spotless uniform and hurried after the head waitress. The staff lined up along the back wall of the dining room as a man no taller than Betsy's five foot two greeted them with lifted nose and hands behind his back.

The creases in his black suit pants looked sharp enough to cut butter. The hard look in his eyes let everyone know there would be no shenanigans or second chances. He stopped in front of Gloria. "There is a speck on your shoe, Miss Burns."

Betsy glanced down to see a slight smudge on the white. She snapped to attention when the manager turned in her direction.

"I am Mr. Dobson. You will call me Mr. Dobson, and you will address each other by your surnames as well. I realize you've been without a manager for a few months, and I am here to remedy the bad habits you have most likely fallen into. We are here to serve and nothing more."

"Sir?" Gloria held herself as rigid as any soldier. "We have several of our military personnel staying here until the pass clears. Some of them are wounded and require extra care, which we've been providing."

"The hotel staff can care for their guests." He sniffed. "While I admire our fighting men and women, we have our own jobs to do."

How would Betsy fulfill her promise of helping Spencer? She could still escort him to his weekly doctor visits on Sundays, but what about his meals? Dr. Cleary didn't have to allow Spencer to make his appointments on Sundays, but since the good doctor oversaw the volunteer program, he allowed it. What if that all changed now?

She wrung her hands under her apron. The time she spent volunteering was one of the highlights of her week. If Mr. Dobson put a stop to all that, Spencer might think she'd abandoned him. Regardless of whether she and Spencer could ever be more than companion and wounded soldier, she didn't want him to think she rejected him.

"Stop fidgeting." Mr. Dobson speared her with a look. He ran the finger of one white-gloved hand down her face. "Very good. Not a trace of makeup.

"Nevertheless, I can see that everyone here needs to be reminded of the Fred Harvey Company rules. I expect everyone to be able to recite them to me by morning. We will meet, just like this, every morning at five o'clock, so I may go over any concerns I may have before the first trainload of customers arrive or the hotel guests trickle in at six. I will also take a look at the work schedule. There may be changes coming. That will be all for now." He gave a sharp wave of his hand.

Betsy met Gloria's startled gaze, then headed for the kitchen. One way or another, Betsy would not give up her Sunday day off. She had a little over a month left on her contract. Surely, the new manager wouldn't make her give up her Sundays and her volunteering.

"Don't worry," Gloria said, following her. "You're one of our best girls."

"I'm not worried about my job performance." Betsy shook out a tablecloth. "I'm concerned with my day off and what I do with that day."

Gloria grabbed one end of the cloth and helped fold. "There might be a reason for concern. I've heard a rumor that Mr. Dobson hates everything about the war because the Germans killed his fiancée, who just happened to be a nurse abroad. If he finds out about your volunteering at the prison hospital, he might revoke your Sundays off."

"Then I'll volunteer on a different day." He couldn't deny her a day off; that would be inhumane. "He doesn't need to know how I spend my free time."

"Miss Burns." Mr. Dobson entered the kitchen. "The

girls are quite capable of folding on their own. If you help them, you foster the unrealistic expectations that you are their friend rather than their supervisor."

"Yes, sir." Gloria handed her end of the tablecloth to Betsy and stepped back. "I'll oversee the dining room now, sir."

He glared at Betsy for several seconds before turning on his heel and leaving the room. She released the breath she was holding and sagged against the counter. Once he found out about Camp Carson, she'd have a bull's eye on her back for sure.

The train whistle blew, signaling the start of a busy day. Betsy headed to her post and stood at attention. Spencer took a seat at one of the tables in her assigned area. Good. Maybe she'd have the opportunity to alert him to the fact she could no longer spend as much time with him. Then she remembered his telegram. She'd have no time to send it now.

Once the train passengers were seated, she made her rounds, taking orders and placing cups in the proper position so the drink girls knew what the customer wanted to drink. When she arrived at Spencer's table, he glanced up at her with a smile. "I was hoping I'd be seated at your table. You didn't come get me this morning."

Betsy glanced over her shoulder. "The new manager wouldn't let me. He said that is the hotel staff's job. I'll still escort you on my days off, but that's all I can manage. Also, about the telegram—"

"Don't worry. I've decided to use the phone and call my parents."

"That is wonderful to hear." Her irritation at him from the day before melted like the snow in spring. She jotted down his order of steak and eggs and rushed to the kitchen under the sharp eye of Mr. Dobson. She'd worked hard every day since being hired by the Harvey Company, but she suspected the days were going to get tougher and a lot less pleasant.

"Miss." One of her customers hailed her the moment she stepped from the kitchen. "I ordered toast with my eggs." The woman pointed at the toast-empty plate in front of her.

"My apologies." Betsy whirled to fetch the toast, coming nose-to-nose with Mr. Dobson.

"Is this a habit, Miss Colter?"

"Is what, sir?"

"Your blunder with the customer's order?" He squared his shoulders. "Most of our customers are on a tight schedule. They can't afford mistakes. Even the hotel guests and those driving by automobile deserve our best service."

Not that there were many automobile or hotel guests because of the deep snow, but she agreed. "Yes, sir."

"Also, please do not spend too much time with one guest. The soldier you carried on a conversation with—"

"He's blind, sir, and needs extra assistance."

Mr. Dobson frowned. "Be careful that your nurturing feminine nature doesn't have you overstepping the boundaries of morality."

What century did the man live in? The man would have a fit with the way the girls flirted and kissed the departing soldiers. All in innocent fun of course. Every soldier needed a smile before heading into danger. Somehow, she knew Mr. Dobson wouldn't understand. "I'll be careful."

"See that you are." He marched away, leaving Betsy and the cook aides staring at each other.

The chef shrugged and returned to slicing ham. "Thanksgiving should be a blast."

Betsy giggled and grabbed the toast, which would have been delivered sooner if the manager hadn't stopped to lecture her. With a fervent apology, she handed the toast to the customer and headed to Spencer's table.

"Since you are no longer allowed to assist me," he said. "Could you find someone to fetch me a hotel maid? I'd like to make the phone call now."

"I'll do my best. Stay here." Her gaze met Mr. Dobson's. "On second thought, take my arm and I'll steer you there. The manager already thinks I spend too much time with you, what's a few seconds more?"

"Would you like me to speak with him?"

"Heavens, no. Thank you, but I'll fight my own battles." She steered him along the wall. "Follow this to the door and turn right. Since you can see some things now, you'll be fine." She patted his shoulder and hurried back to the kitchen.

"That man insists I speak to you about not following orders," Gloria said, her arms crossed. "So consider yourself spoken to."

Betsy sighed. "I've done nothing wrong." Except for the toast, which she suspected the manager would hang over her head for days, if not weeks. She leaned against the counter. "He had me send Spencer on his way alone. I steered the poor man along the wall like a blind dog." Tears stung her eyes.

"You really care for this soldier, don't you?"

"No." Betsy shook her head hard enough to loosen

her hair from its bun. "I've sworn off any type of romantic notions about military men." Right? Oh, no. Her shoulders slumped. She'd stepped over the line and come to care far too much for Spencer.

What in the world was she going to do?

*

Things were changing at the hotel and not for the better. Good thing Spencer could see well enough not to run into walls and doors, but he didn't appreciate the fact Betsy seemed afraid to be around him. Despite her refusal, he intended to speak with the new manager at his first opportunity. Right after he made the call home.

At the front desk, he had the operator patch him through to Waldon's General Store. "Mr. Waldon? This is Spencer Gregory. I'm wondering whether you could get a message to my parents?"

"Spencer! Why don't you give me a call back in an hour and speak to them yourself? Won't take me but a bit to go fetch them." The man's jovial voice boomed across the line.

Did he want to speak with his mother and hear her tearful voice remind him of why she didn't want him to be a military doctor?

"They think you're dead, boy," Mr. Waldon said. "With months passing with no word..."

"I've been in the hospital, but please don't tell them that. I'll explain everything when I call. I'm doing fine now, but the pass is blocked."

"You call back. They'll be here." *Click.*

Spencer handed the phone back to the clerk with his thanks. What would he do for the next hour? Doing nothing other than listen to people pass by on the way about their daily lives was growing tedious. He sat on a plush velvet-covered divan, trusting the hotel clerk would let him know when an hour was up.

What if he volunteered at the military hospital? Maybe Betsy was right, and he could help by listening to the patient's ailments. With the help of a nurse, he could do more than he thought, most likely. But he'd insist on helping only the American patients. Oath or not, he couldn't bring himself to save the life of a German soldier. Not yet, anyway. Maybe never.

"Clerk? Please let me know if you see the restaurant manager." He might as well deal with that unpleasant task while waiting for the time to pass.

"I'll fetch him for you, sir." The man's footsteps pounded away.

Spencer rested his elbow on the armrest and plopped his chin in his hand. He definitely needed to find something to fill his days.

"You wished to speak with me, sir. I'm the manager, Mr. Dobson."

Spencer got to his feet and thrust out his hand. When the other man didn't reciprocate the gesture, he folded his hands behind his back. "You may not be aware of the fact, sir, but I am almost completely blind. My doctor has enlisted the service of one of your girls to be my eyes. She has told me that she is no longer able to do so, at your request."

"That is correct."

"May I inquire why?"

The man sniffed. "The waitresses have jobs to do, sir. Jobs they are paid to do by the Harvey Company. We are here to provide a service, but not to individuals. If you require assistance, I suggest you hire a companion or ask the hotel staff to assist you. Have a good day, sir." The man's heels beat a sharp regular tempo across the floor as he retreated. Spencer couldn't see him but he'd guess the man held himself as stiffly as if he had a board down the back of his shirt.

The desk phone rang, startling Spencer. He whirled, swayed, and got himself on the edge of the sofa.

"The phone is for you, Mr. Gregory."

He crossed the room. His folks must not have wanted to wait. Spencer grabbed the phone. "Hello?"

His mother burst into tears. "It is you."

He smiled. "Who did you expect?"

"Not my son back from the dead."

"I was never dead, Ma. I was wounded, and spent some time in a hospital in France, but I'm fine now. I'm staying at the El Otero until the pass clears and I'm seeing one of the doctors at Camp Carson."

"If you're fine, why are you still seeing a doctor? What happened?"

Typical Ma to want to know all the details. "I hit my head. It's only a precaution. They'd like me to stay just a bit longer." He closed his eyes, not wanting to upset her. He needed to be more careful with his words. "Don't worry about me. I wanted to let you know I'm fine, and to wish you and Pop a happy Thanksgiving."

"It's a happy one now." She sniffed, and Spencer knew she cried tears of happiness. "Here's your father."

"How you holding up, son?"

Spencer leaned against the wall, the warmth of his father's voice wrapping around him like a trusty blanket. "I'm good."

"Had a tough time over there?"

"I'm not in a hurry to go back." That was the truth!

"Want me to hitch up the sleigh and come get you?

Might take me a couple of days, but I can manage."

Spencer chuckled. "I'll see you in the spring, Pop, but you can reach me on the phone here if you need me."

"Good to know, son. God bless and happy Thanksgiving. Thanks for calling. We love you."

His father hung up the phone a split hair's second before Spencer could return the sentiment. Obviously his folks were relieved and excited that he was back in the United States. The phone conversation lifted his spirits, too, and now he had until the spring to pray his eyesight fully returned before he made his way home.

As soon as he stepped back into the dining room, he caught a whiff of Betsy's familiar rosewater scent. He breathed deep and waited to be seated for lunch. Since his day seemed to revolve around meal times, he'd gain ten pounds or more before spring. He requested Betsy's section again and followed the hostess to the end of the long table.

"We don't have an empty solitary table, sir. We're full today," she said.

"This is fine." He squeezed in between two young men in navy uniforms.

Their excitement at being shipped overseas tore at his heart. He wanted to set them straight and explain the realities of war. But who was he to damper their enthusiasm? Instead, he said a prayer for their safety and grinned. Somehow, without him knowing, God had snuck back into his life with each small step forward in Spencer regaining his sight.

"What can I get for you, Spencer?" Betsy appeared at his elbow.

"I'll take the broiled chicken." He handed her the

menu. "I overheard the other fellows talking. I still can't see well enough to read."

She patted his shoulder. "You will. I have faith."

"Before you go, I wanted to let you know I called my parents."

"And?"

"They thought I was dead. You were right. I should have called them a long time ago."

"Did you tell them about your lack of sight?"

"No." He hung his head. "I couldn't. I'll tell them in the spring."

"Oh, Spencer." She heaved a sad-sounding sigh "Your pride is going to hurt you someday. I'll go put your order in now."

Someday? His pride was already an open wound beginning to fester.

"That gal is a real doll," one of the navy men said. "She rationed?"

Spencer wanted to say yes, that he'd laid claim to her, but that wouldn't be fair. Who was he to say a woman was his when his future was so uncertain? "No, she's not."

"Great. I'm going to ask her to step out with me tonight. There's a movie playing down the street. I heard *Heaven Can Wait* is a good movie to take a broad to."

Spencer wadded his napkin in his hand to prevent himself from throttling the young man. If Betsy had a desire to go to the movies, he could take her. He could listen to the actors. "I'm sure the movie will be over by the time she gets off work, but you're welcome to try."

"I heard she's off on Sundays. I'll ask her then." The man's fork clattered against his plate. "Catch up to you later, army man."

Betsy returned with Spencer's meal. "I'm so glad to see you out among the living. It wasn't good when you spent all that time in your room."

No, but it was more peaceful. At least then he didn't have to listen to other men regale him with tales of Betsy's beauty. He turned his face up to hers, imagining he could see her guileless blue eyes and lips that always seemed to be curled into a smile. He wanted nothing more at that moment than to pull her into his arms and see whether her kiss was as sweet as he remembered.

"The days are long, Betsy. I need something to do. I'm thinking of volunteering at the hospital."

"That's wonderful. We can use you."

"On the American side."

"Oh." She stepped back. She turned and walked away.

Not everyone could have a heart like Betsy. He shouldn't beat himself up. Yet, her opinion mattered—a lot.

10

The usual clatter of pots and pans and chatter of busy workers was strangely silent on Thanksgiving morning as Betsy slipped into her place in line at 5:00 a.m. She folded her hands behind her back and stared straight ahead while Mr. Dobson marched down the line.

"Very well. Looking good. Let's get this dinner ready." He clapped his hands and then waved them away.

Like birds evading a predator, the workers scattered to their respective posts. Every day was filled with duties, but a holiday provided twice as much work. Still, thanksgiving rose in Betsy's heart. She had much to be grateful for. A good job, a comfortable place to live, the opportunity to minister and show God's love to others, not to mention the opportunity to know Spencer better.

Yes, he might be leaving in a few months and yes,

she'd vow to never fall for another military man, but there was nothing wrong with being friends, was there? Even if the man had a mental block in regards to helping *all* people who needed his skills.

She busied herself covering the tables with starched white tablecloths and sparkling silverware. The long tables were shoved so closely together, she and the other girls would have to move sideways between them once their guests were seated. The restaurant expected more than their usual number of soldiers for the holiday meal, and it was all hands on deck.

By seven o'clock the waitresses served breakfast and by nine, they were clearing the tables again in preparation for the main meal of the day. Betsy swiped the back of her hand across her face. Why couldn't there have been a way of serving breakfast without redoing everything for the Thanksgiving feast?

"Stop dawdling, Miss Colter." Mr. Dobson frowned on his way past. "We've a busy day ahead of us."

"Yes, Mr. Dobson." Betsy wiped some errant bread crumbs into her hand and rushed to the kitchen. After disposing of the crumbs, she grabbed a tray of clean china and hurried out to set the tables. If she kept her eye on the blessing of serving others, she might be able to forget the pain in her feet and the ache in her back.

Once back in the kitchen, she lowered herself gingerly into a chair. Gracious it felt good to sit down. She rarely took a break, but the morning's frantic pace called for one. She leaned her head back and closed her eyes.

The doors to the kitchen banged open. "Get up," Gloria told her. "Dobson is coming and he's on the rampage."

Betsy bolted to her feet. "Why?"

"Someone spilled juice on one of the tablecloths and covered it with a plate instead of replacing the cloth."

Betsy's heart dropped to her feet. "Whose table?"

"Yours." Gloria pressed her lips together and whirled to face the manager as he entered the kitchen and stopped just inside the door.

"Miss Colter." He shook his head. "Your negligence has cost you a point."

"But sir—" A point? Really? Since when had they returned to the old way of ranking the waitresses?

"There are no excuses. Replace the tablecloth immediately." He spun and ran into Spencer, who was entering the room.

"Sir. I spilled the juice." He stood at military attention. "I thought I had cleaned it all up and put the dishes back where they belonged. I'm willing to help in other ways if I've set the girls back in any way."

"You've done enough, soldier." Mr. Dobson set his jaw. "How, exactly, do you expect a blind man to help ready a restaurant for a large meal? Good day, sir."

High spots of color appeared on Spencer's cheeks.

"Don't pay him any attention." Betsy rushed to his side. "You can be plenty of help, if you still want to. There's a ton of silverware to be rolled." She grabbed his hand. Jolts of electricity ran up her arm. Had she ever touched his skin before? No, she'd always looped her arm with his or had a layer of clothing between them. She jerked back. "Let me get that for you."

Goodness, she needed to be careful if she didn't want to be a total wreck when he left. She gathered the napkins and silverware. "You can tell by touch how to do them. Give a yell if you have a question. One of us will be around to help you."

"Thank you."

She grabbed a fresh table cloth and headed for the door. She stopped. "Why?"

"Why what?" He faced her.

"Why do you want to help?"

"I've nothing to do. The boredom is killing me." He shrugged. "Besides, my clumsiness got you in trouble. Helping is the least I can do."

"Thank you." She shouldn't be catty, just because her views were different from his on helping the German POWs. After all, Spencer was the one who had fought for their freedom and come home injured.

She cast one more look over her shoulder before leaving the kitchen. His dark head was bent over his task, his strong shoulders bowed over the table. By the way his fingers moved, bending the napkins to his will, she suspected he could see enough for the chore.

So much time had passed, she'd forgotten what it felt like to have those sky-blue eyes of his focus on her face. Sure, they were still beautiful, but they lacked the intensity with which he'd stared into her face before boarding the train to take him away. Would she ever experience that thrill again? Would his look send her pulse racing the way it had when she'd touched his hand?

She pushed through the door. One of the other girls had cleared the table, leaving it empty for Betsy. She shook out the tablecloth.

Were her growing feelings for the Spencer she knew now, or the one she'd fallen for over their months of correspondence? A life with a man bitter because of his injury would be a hard life indeed. Still, she sometimes wondered whether she was strong enough to be only a companion to him. She could not renew her contract and also escort him to his next destination—if he wanted her. But how would she know whether he wanted her because he loved her or because she was of use to him?

Once she had the cloth smooth, she replaced the dishes and added vases of greenery to the center of the table, placing them a few feet apart until they stood in a straight line like soldiers. She stepped back and admired her work.

"Nice touch, Miss Colter," Mr. Dobson said. "Do the rest of the tables the same."

She fought the urge to roll her eyes. Of course she'd do the other tables. The room wouldn't look right if she didn't. "Yes, sir." She rushed to locate more vases and to check on Spencer.

He had quite a pile in front of him. "You'll make a Harvey girl yet," she said, smiling.

He laughed. "No, thank you. You gals work too hard. Give me blood and broken bones any day." He stood and stretched. "Besides, sitting over that table will give me a permanent hump. What else can I do?"

"Hmm." She tilted her head. Every chore she gave him, no matter how small, increased his independence. "I'm searching for vases. Once I find them, you can set up the other tables the same way as the first. You might have to feel your way a bit, but I'm confident you'll do fine." She stepped into a large supply closet.

"You have more confidence in my abilities than most people." He moved toward her until only a hair's breadth separated them.

Betsy glanced around the kitchen. They were alone.

His body heat radiated through his uniform. He was going to kiss her, and she wouldn't stop him. All she could do was pray no one barged in and caught them.

"Why are you so sweet, Betsy Colter? What in your life made you always look on the rosy side of things?" He slipped his hands around her waist, stealing her breath.

She needed to breathe. That's all. Just take one breath and then another. "Um." The answer was God. Why couldn't she speak?

He lowered his head and placed his lips against hers. This wasn't the sweet goodbye kiss of months ago. This was the kiss of a starving man. His soft lips claimed hers. His strong hands cupped her head. Betsy's knees went weak. She snaked her arms around his neck. They should quit. Someone would come. But, oh, he felt nice.

Her senses returned. No. She pushed him back. "I'll get fired." It would be worth it. She stared at his lips. No. Her job was all she had. Oh, she wanted to be kissed again.

*

Spencer grinned and stepped back. The quickening of her breath quickened his pulse. He wanted to grab her close again, but she was right. If they were caught... He stood right outside the closet and leaned against the doorjamb. There would be other opportunities to steal a kiss.

"Stop looking at me like that."

"Like what?" He quirked the corner of his mouth.

"Like I'm a bowl of strawberries and cream."

"Oh, you're more delicious than that, doll." He moved aside so she could pass.

"Here are the vases." Her voice sounded shaky. "Set

them out and I'll find something to put in them." She sailed away, leaving a trail of rose scent in her wake.

"Careful, man. A broad like that will leave you scorched." The chef waved a wooden spoon.

A spoon? Spencer grinned. His sight had become clearer still. Maybe he'd see the flush on Betsy's cheeks the next time he kissed her, after all. At the rate his vision was improving, the chances were very good. Happy Thanksgiving, Private First Class Gregory. "I'm hoping to be set on fire."

The man's laughter followed Spencer into the dining room. The blurry scene in front of him convinced him that he'd ask for a pair of spectacles at his next doctor's appointment. He wasn't too vain to wear eyeglasses, especially if they might improve his vision to where he could actually see people's expressions. There was one very important person whose face he most desired to see clearly.

She laughed from the far side of the room, drawing him to her like a horse to a sugar cube. Sergeant Harris responded in kind, halting Spencer's progress across the floor. Of course the man would attend the Thanksgiving dinner. What a fool Spencer was to think he'd have Betsy to himself.

But what about their kiss? Well, his kiss. She hadn't responded for a second or two, and he definitely hadn't asked for permission. A gal like Betsy shouldn't have to wait around for the possibility of his vision to return. He couldn't ask her to. He shoved his hand in his pocket where he still carried her handkerchief. Maybe, if she were still around when he was once again a whole man, he'd pursue a relationship. Until then, no more kissing, no matter how enticed he was.

Heart heavy, Spencer took a seat in another girl's section for the first time. Although there were other items on the menu, he handed it to the waitress without trying to see the words. It was Thanksgiving, and as such, he'd have the turkey and stuffing.

"I'd like to speak to you after you've eaten," Betsy said as she marched past.

Her harsh tone told Spencer he might want to run rather than meet with her. But he wasn't a coward. He'd face the little gal's wrath with squared shoulders.

Soon the dining room filled with friendly chatter and the enticing aroma of roasted turkey, rich gravy and fresh-baked rolls. Spencer ate with gusto. He'd need his strength when he met with Betsy. What could have her ire up? Was she upset about the kiss now that she'd had time to think about it?

He hoped not. While he planned to keep his lips away from hers, he still had a few months to stay at the hotel and didn't want tension between them. He took a bite of fluffy mashed potatoes that were every bit as good as his ma's.

Thinking of his parents sent a pain through his heart. He should have contacted them immediately upon arriving. It hadn't been fair to worry them. One more thing to add to his long list of self-pity and immaturity. At thirty years old, Spencer was a grown man, a doctor, a skilled military personnel trained to save lives.

He dropped his fork beside his plate. Instead of being the man God wanted him to be, despite what was proving to be a temporary handicap, he'd wallowed in self-pity and anger and quite possibly hurt the feelings of one of the finest women he'd ever have the fortune to meet. He bowed his head to pray and give thanks.

Better late than never, or so the saying went.

After prayer, he shoved back his chair and went in search of Betsy. One of the other girls said she'd gone into the kitchen. Not seeing the manager, Spencer thought it wise to wait outside the door rather than hunt her down. She had to come out at some time.

By the time she made her appearance, his nerves were on edge. "I thought you'd gone to your room."

"The staff is allowed a break to eat, Spencer. Follow me." She led the way to a small alcove off the dining room. She took a deep breath. "Are you toying with me?"

"Excuse me?" He frowned.

"First, you kiss me without permission, and then you then sit in someone else's area. Are you playing with my affections? Are you so bored waiting for the snow to melt that you will pass the time with kisses? Because if you are, you can stop it. Please do not kiss me again. I have no desire to become entangled with a military man."

"Not even Sergeant Harris?" What if she did prefer the other man over Spencer?

"Not even him. The attention is nice, but it is also my job to be pleasant and my duty as a Christian to be kind.."

My, she was feisty. "What would you do if I were to kiss you right now?" He wanted to, very badly.

"I'll sock you." She poked him in the chest with her finger. "I'm very happy that your sight is returning because right now, I'm ready to leave you to your own devices."

He grabbed her hand. "Please, don't. I enjoy the small amount of time we spend together."

"Good day, Spencer. We'll see whether I'm still angry on Sunday." She stormed away.

He fought the laugh bubbling inside. It had bothered her that he didn't sit in her section. That knowledge sent a wave of pleasure through him. He'd visit the commissary on Sunday and buy her some flowers. That should soften her attitude toward him. Maybe he'd use a precious rationed coupon and purchase some chocolates.

If he did, would she think he was courting her? He slumped against the wall. Was he toying with her in an attempt to relieve his boredom? He wasn't that big of a fathead, was he? No wonder she had a beef with him. He needed to apologize pronto.

He rushed into the dining room and waited to hear her voice. He wished he could spot her with his eyes, but all the girls looked the same to him in their white dresses. To his right came her musical laugh, followed once again by the deeper one of Sergeant Harris's. Christian kindness or not, the man seemed to like Betsy for more than a casual friend. Each laugh of his was like shards of glass into Spencer's heart. Maybe Betsy wasn't being entirely truthful when she said she didn't want a relationship with a military man. Maybe it was only him.

Deciding against a slice of pie, he headed back to his room. Once there, he called down to the front desk and requested a magnifying glass in hopes that he could read Betsy's letters with it. He really wanted to read the one that had disappeared from his bureau. Had she taken it back? Why? What had she written that she no longer wanted him to see? What if someone else had taken it? Should he report it stolen?

He frowned. He could have knocked it to the floor. Perhaps it lay under the dresser at this very moment. Still, his gut told him Betsy had taken it in order to prevent him from reading something she no longer wanted him to see.

When the magnifying glass arrived, he retrieved the bundle of letters and sat in the chair beside the small table in one corner of the room. He held the glass over the cursive words, and smiled. He could read again. Tears stung his eyes, blurring his name on the envelope. With the aid of spectacles, he could resume his role of a doctor. Maybe not in active duty on the front line, but in a military hospital or in civilian service.

He covered his face and wept.

11

Betsy peered around the corner at a deep-in-thought Spencer. In his hand, he held the handkerchief she'd given him months ago. His fingers caressed the soft fabric. Occasionally, he brought the embroidered square to his nose. He'd kept it. Tears stung her eyes. Did that mean she was more than someone to pass the time with?

She stepped back to prevent anyone from spotting her spying and plastered her back to the wall. Had she been wrong on Thursday about him toying with her? Did she want him to look at her as anything other than a diversion? She'd avoided him since Thanksgiving, not giving him a chance to explain or cajole her with sugary words. Now, it was Sunday and time for her to escort him to the hospital.

"Bye, Gloria, see you in a few hours." Gloria was nowhere to be seen, but Betsy wanted to give Spencer warning that she was coming.

He stood when she entered the hotel's foyer and shoved her handkerchief into his pocket. He crooked his arm with a smile. "Ready?"

"You're chipper this morning." She slipped her arm in his.

"I may have a surprise for you after my appointment."

"Really?" Excitement leaped within her. "I love surprises."

They chattered on the way to the train platform as if the emotions of Thursday had never happened, discussing the unusually cold weather and deep snow which continued to block the pass. They compared the uptight Mr. Dobson with the congenial Gloria, and laughed at the antics of the servicemen who passed through the doors of the hotel. By the time the train stopped so they could hitch a ride to Camp Carson, Betsy's face hurt from grinning. She'd never enjoyed Spencer's company more.

This was the companionship she craved. Time spent with a man who could make her laugh, who looked at her as if she were the only girl on the train, and listened to every word she spoke as if they held the utmost importance. The only problem with Spencer, or any soldier, treating her this way was the way her heart melted, and that would never do. Someday, God would send her a man to love that didn't wear a uniform. A man she could trust.

Sergeant Harris met her at the gate. "Betsy, Doctor, I've a bit of news for you."

"Good news, I hope." Betsy shifted the basket on her arm.

"Let me carry that for you." He took the basket. "Dr. Cleary has come down with pneumonia. While the doctor handling the wounded American soldiers is handling his appointments, the prisoners have suffered a bit from lack of attention." He frowned down at her. "I'm afraid you've a rather busy afternoon ahead of you."

"I can handle hard work." What would she find in the prisoner ward? Hopefully the nurses had been able to tend to the most important needs. "We'd best hurry, then." She turned to the silent man beside her. "Spencer, will you wait for me in the lobby?"

"Of course I will." He tipped his hat at the sergeant and rushed away from them.

"His eyesight seems to be returning," Sergeant Harris said.

"Not as fast as he would like, I'm afraid." Betsy increased her pace, in a hurry to see what needed to be done. "I think he was hoping for good news today, but with Dr. Cleary ill…well, I don't know what he'll hear."

"Don't worry about the chap. He's tough enough to handle things."

Maybe so, but was Betsy strong enough to handle Spencer's dashed hopes? As his friend, she wanted only the best for him. She sent a prayer heavenward as Sergeant Harris opened the door to the hospital and ushered her through.

She stepped into chaos. Nurses rushed to and fro, their arms overloaded with bedding, buckets and cleaning supplies. One of them stopped and thrust the bucket into Betsy's hands. "Thank God you're here. We can't minister medicine to the patients when there's, well, stuff to clean up. You'll want an apron and gloves." She hurried off, leaving Betsy with her mouth hanging open.

She would read to the patients, write their letters, fluff their pillows and carry on conversations to ease their loneliness. She didn't do "stuff." Especially the smelly stuff she feared the nurse was talking about. She glanced up at Sergeant Harris's pale face. He shook his head and dashed outside.

So much for chivalry. She straightened her shoulders and headed for the supply closet to don an apron and gloves. Once she was suited for battle, she headed toward the sound of moans and retching. Outside the door to the prisoner wing she took a deep breath—and gagged. She turned and sprinted back to the closet for a surgical mask. With tears in her eyes and fortitude in her steps, she marched back to the patients and thrust open the door. She could do this.

Within minutes, she was changing soiled bedding. After that, she moved to mopping floors. The flu seemed to have attacked every patient. Exhaustion lined the nurses' faces. Betsy resolved not to complain about the nasty work. She was only here for a few hours. The nurses had been working for days with minimal staffing.

She stopped to rest and leaned against a table. She brushed hair that had fallen from its bun away from her face with the back of her hand. The door to the infirmary opened and two soldiers marched in, wearing masks and doctor's robes over their fatigues. They gave her a nod and set to work, doing in half the time what it had taken Betsy all afternoon to accomplish. When they headed back for the door, she stopped them.

"Wait. Thank you for doing this."

"We had no choice, ma'am. We were only following orders." The hard glint in his eyes told her he would not have helped had he been given the choice.

"It's still the Christian thing to do. God bless you."

"We'll be back in two hours." He nodded, and the two left.

She wished she could erase the hatred in the world as efficiently as she could scrub the day's grime off the floor. She wished a lot of things. That Spencer would help with the short-staffed prisoners ward, that God would restore Spencer's sight, that the war would end. None seemed as if they'd come true anytime soon. Her shoulders slumped, and her spirit sagged. Could a few really make a difference in the grand scheme of things?

The Bible said they could, but on days like today, Betsy's faith faltered. Maybe foregoing church each Sunday to minister to the sick and imprisoned wasn't such a good idea. She needed to find a way to balance the two. But the train left the station before church services were over. Could she take the time every other Sunday to have her own soul ministered to when there were others who didn't know the Lord at all?

Her questions kept her company while she cleaned. Occasionally, she'd stop to say a kind word, to give a smile, but most of her time was spent cleaning up after the sick and running errands for the harried nurses. By the time the end of her shift came, her feet ached, her back hurt and she desperately needed a bath.

"You are a blessing, Miss Colter," one of the nurses said. "I wish you could come more often."

Betsy gave a tired smile. "I doubt my boss would approve. He's a stickler about the rules." She left out the fact the man didn't know how Betsy spent her Sundays and that he would most definitely not approve.

"All the same, you're a blessing from God, and there's no denying it." The nurse plopped into a chair. "I'm Alice. I thought joining the army would be glamorous, and I'd have the chance to see the world."

"I'm Betsy." She laughed. "I thought the same about working for the Harvey Company. The closest we've gotten to anything new and exotic was the German language."

"Would you like some coffee?" Alice stood. "Come with me to the cafeteria. You've time before the train leaves."

"I'd love to, as long as there is a place to sit down."

"There are comfortable chairs."

Betsy discarded her apron and gloves, then followed the nurse down two flights of stairs and entered a room that echoed with the voices of lunching nurses, doctors and visitors, and the clank of dishes. Why weren't some of these medical personnel helping with the prisoner wing?

"I know what you're thinking," Alice said, staring at a spot over Betsy's shoulder. "Don't get all worked up over it. The military people follow orders. That's it. I was furious about my assignment for a few weeks, then I realized these poor men are no different than our own boys in khaki. It takes some folks longer, but they'll eventually see the light."

They grabbed their coffee from a small counter off to one side, and Betsy followed the cheerful blond nurse to a round table in the center of the room. Alice was right. Betsy should have known these people couldn't up and work in one wing while assigned somewhere else.

"My my, that is one good-looking soldier." Alice glanced toward the door.

Betsy glanced over her shoulder. Spencer stood in the doorway, a grin directed toward her. On his face was a pair of gold-rimmed glasses.

*

After waiting three hours for a doctor to get free long enough to keep Spencer's appointment and give him an eye exam, Spencer walked out with a new pair of glasses. The world in all its clarity and beauty waited for him. With time to spare before the train, he'd headed to the cafeteria for a cup of coffee and a sandwich. The last person he expected to see was the ever lovely Betsy. She was more beautiful than he remembered, even with her auburn hair falling from its bun.

He ignored every other face in the room and made a beeline for her table. "Hello."

"You can see." Betsy's breathless words sent his pulse into overdrive.

"Crystal clear." He pulled out a chair and sat, reaching across the table for her hand. "The doctor thinks these eyeglasses may be only temporary, and that my eyesight will fully return in time."

"That's wonderful."

"I'm Alice." The other gal thrust out her hand.

"Spencer Gregory, Private First Class."

"I'm also the fifth wheel. Enjoy your coffee. See you next Sunday, Betsy." She tossed them a wave and joined two nurses and a nearby table.

"Are they putting you back on duty?" Betsy blew into her coffee.

Spencer dragged his gaze away from her pursed lips. "Not yet. Within a couple of weeks, though."

"Great." Her eyes sparkled. "We need your help desperately in the prison wing. With the flu hitting so hard, the nurses and volunteers are so busy, we don't know which end is up. It would mean so much to me."

"I've got to get something to eat." He shoved back his chair and rushed to the counter. Instead of being thrilled that he could see, she only wanted him to help the last people he wanted to spend time with. What was her deal?

He paid for his meal and headed back to Betsy. "Did you want something to eat?"

"No, thanks. Not after what I've been cleaning up." She shuddered.

His heart sank, taking in the fatigue in the line of her shoulders. "Hard day?"

"The worst, but you don't want to hear about my day." Her smile trembled. "Congratulations on the glasses. You look very distinguished."

Did she have to make him feel like such a jerk? He shoved his plate away and straightened in his chair. "I'm sorry. I seem to be constantly hurting your feelings."

"Not at all. You're entitled to your opinion." She sipped her drink.

Why did she have to be so sweet when he was so surly? "It's hard for me to look at the Germans as anything other than the enemy."

"I understand."

She didn't, though. He could tell by her downturned expression. Not having been at war, not having seen what the German bullets did to young men who once had excitement in their eyes, not having seen bodies so mangled they didn't fill a body bag, she had no idea. He didn't want her to know the horrors of war. He wanted only flowers and sunshine for Betsy. Giving her an affirmative answer would brighten her day. Still, he fought against giving in.

He wanted to save American lives, and the lives of America's allies. Not their enemies.

"Are you a Christian, Spencer?" Betsy's eyes shimmered with unshed tears.

"Yes." Please, don't cry. If her tears escaped, he'd promise her anything.

"Doesn't God ask us to love our enemy? To turn the other cheek?" She stood and held out her hand. "Come with me."

"I can't take your hand. We're on base." But he wanted nothing more than to touch her silky skin.

"Come." She wiggled her fingers.

Knowing he'd follow her to the moon and back, he let her lead the way to the prison wing. They didn't speak. The only sound between them was the sound of their shoes against the polished tile floor. The smell of antiseptic and sickness greeted them well before Betsy opened the infirmary doors.

"Step inside. See what I'm talking about." She blinked. Tears clung to her eyelashes like tiny diamonds.

At the risk of receiving a demerit for public display of affection, Spencer wiped them away with his finger. "Okay." He lifted his chin and stepped into where Betsy spent her one day off a week.

Nurses scurried like mice, one exhausted doctor dashed from patient to patient, the beds were filled with moaning men, and over it all hung a cloud of despair. A fist gripped his heart, and he stared down at Betsy. "You win. I can't leave after seeing this. Enemy or not, no man deserves to find healing in such conditions."

"We've an hour until the train." She grinned. "I'll fetch you a coat."

He chuckled and shook his head. The little minx. How could he resist her tears and seeing all this? If Betsy could spend her Sundays here, then so could he. The plus side would be working alongside her.

He marched down the aisle between the beds until he reached the doctor. He thrust out his hand. "Private First Class Gregory at your service. I'm a doctor on medical leave for another week or two. I have an hour today, then I'll return in the morning."

"Thank God." He handed Spencer a clipboard. "Could you check on these patients? Just tell the nurses what you need. I'm Dr. Lincoln." Beads of sweat glistened across the man's forehead. "Wear a mask. This room is full of death."

Betsy rushed forward with a mask, gloves and a surgical coat. "Thank you, Spencer. I'll wait for you in the lobby. I can't work anymore today. I'm too tired."

Other than flu symptoms, which Spencer could do little to relieve other than hand out aspirin and cold compresses, the patients didn't seem too bad off. If Betsy hadn't coerced him to visit the wing on a day when the flu was prevalent, he doubted he would have stepped forward to offer his services.

The patients eyed him with suspicion and distrust. He treated them with cold detachment. Both parties seemed satisfied with the outcome when Spencer moved on. Maybe they could sense his reluctance to ease their pain. Still, Betsy was right. It was what God would want him to do, and hadn't God healed Spencer's eyesight? Ministering to the enemy was a small price to pay—not to mention a fulfillment of his Hippocratic Oath.

He'd been so close a few times to stepping in front of a train. Now, he had purpose again. He actually looked forward to the snow melting and him going home for a short furlough. Maybe he could take Betsy with him. Ma would love her.

Slumped in a chair in the lobby, her woven basket at her feet, slept Betsy. What would she do if Spencer woke her with a kiss? He glanced around to see whether they were alone. If holding hands could get him in trouble, a kiss sure would.

Instead, he knelt in front of her and took her hands in his. "Betsy? Sweetheart?"

Her eyes fluttered open. "I fell asleep."

"You deserved it. I'm bushed after only an hour." He helped her up and looped her basket over his arm.

The doors opened and Sergeant Harris breezed in.

"I've got her, buddy." Spencer grinned, put his hand on the small of Betsy's back and escorted her out the door. The man could find himself someone else. This pretty gal belonged to Spencer.

12

"Great news," Gloria said as Betsy entered the dining room before the evening meal. "Mr. Dobson is gone and soon to be replaced."

Betsy grinned and started making coffee. "How did that happen?"

"The dear soldiers complained about his attitude and scorn. Since these boys are defending our country, the Harvey Company wanted nothing more to do with him. We're having a dance after dinner to celebrate."

"Here?" She glanced around the crowded room. Where would they put all the tables and chairs?

"Sure. We'll just pile everything against the walls and stack the chairs. It'll be fun." Gloria winked and sashayed into the kitchen, her rounded hips rotating like a whirlygig. She tossed over her shoulder that she might actually find a husband at the dance.

Betsy smiled inwardly. Why was she even thinking

about marriage? Had words of love passed her lips or Spencer's? She knew the answers only too well. Because he was the handsomest man she'd ever laid eyes on and his kisses made her forget all reason, that's why. Not to mention his kindness, sensitive nature and patience. Well, he was patient most of the time.

Coffee brewing, she checked the tablecloths for stains and made sure napkins and silverware were set beside each place setting. Once the tables filled, there'd be little time for double-checking the little niceties and luxuries the hotel was known for. Despite the war rationing, the restaurant strived to make its customers forget the atrocities and enjoy a fine meal. From some of the stories Betsy had heard from the soldiers, they deserved to forget for a while.

Gloria returned and set a gramophone in the corner. "This will be such fun!"

Her excitement was contagious, and Betsy practically skipped through the rest of her predinner chores. Gloria had said they would still need to wear their uniforms unless off duty, but Betsy didn't care. What could be better than the chance to dance and have fun and to brighten the lives of soldiers heading off to war?

As dinner wore on, Betsy kept an eye out for Spencer. By the time things were cleared and tables shoved aside, he had yet to make an appearance. She tossed her apron in the laundry bin and headed upstairs. Maybe he was ill or maybe he had decided to stay on base for the evening. Since he chose to spend his days at the hospital now that the glasses were correcting his vision, Betsy rarely saw him. It wasn't until he stopped dogging her steps at the hotel that she realized how much seeing him each day had come to mean to her.

The mournful sound of a harmonica drifted down the hall. Betsy stopped in front of Spencer's room and put her ear to the door. She didn't know he played. He'd never mentioned it in his letters. She listened for several minutes. She didn't recognize the song, only the heartbreak in the notes.

She knocked, and the music stopped. She stepped back and waited for Spencer to open the door. He did, standing there in stocking feet and rumpled uniform, with his hair standing on end. "Are you okay? You haven't come down with the flu, have you?"

"No, I'm fine. Just tired." He cocked his head. "Can I do something for you?"

"We're having a dance downstairs. It's sort of an impromptu thing, but I'd like you to come."

He exhaled sharply, his features set in hard lines. "I'm too tired for dancing, but thank you for asking me." He started to close the door.

"Wait. Have I done something to upset you?"

"No." He ran his hand through his hair, mussing it further. "I've got a lot on my mind and it's been a long week. I hope you understand."

She shoved her hands into the pockets of her dress and struggled to keep the disappointment at bay. "The harmonica sounded beautiful. I'd like to hear it again sometime." She stepped back. "Have a good evening, Spencer." She whirled and dashed away before he could see her cry.

She reentered the dining room to the jazzy tune of "Boogie Woogie Bugle Boy." A soldier immediately swept her into a jitter bug. After that song she danced with another soldier to "G.I. Jive." The poor man's elbows and knees seemed to fly everywhere. Still,

Betsy laughed until her face hurt. She couldn't remember having so much fun. The floor vibrated from dancing feet, and soon other hotel guests joined the Harvey girls and the soldiers. For a couple of hours, people were able to forget the war.

But Betsy couldn't forget Spencer. As a slow song started, she bowed out and headed for a cup of tea to soothe her parched throat. She laughed at the antics of Gloria and an especially clumsy G.I. who danced with enthusiasm if not skill. Maybe the happy-go-lucky head waitress had found her charming soldier after all. When a slow song had the two locked in an embrace so tight light couldn't shine between them, Betsy was convinced.

While happy for her friend, her heart ached. She glanced repeatedly toward the stairs, hoping Spencer would decide to join the party.

The music had slowed again, and she was glad to not have a partner. The intimacy of the slower songs left her uncomfortable. Especially when her partner wanted kisses and whispered promises she couldn't give him. She'd played that game with Spencer on a train once upon a time and look where it had left her. Alone at a party.

"May I have this dance?"

She turned and stared into Spencer's freshly shaved face. The scent of his after-shave, something new and musky she hadn't smelled before, assaulted her senses. His smile made her knees weak.

"Please?" He held out a hand. "I'm sorry I was disgruntled. My mind is so full of my daily duties, I can think of little else."

"Maybe I can help you forget, if only for a while."

She slipped her hand in his.

He swung her onto the floor as "As Time Goes By" softly played. She rested her cheek against his solid chest and closed her eyes. No matter how hard she fought against it, Spencer stole another piece of her heart every time he looked at her.

*

After an overwhelming day of emotions while helping at the hospital, the last thing Spencer wanted to do was dance. But the sorrowful look on Betsy's lovely face when he'd turned her down had ripped at his heart and before he realized what he was doing, he had changed his clothes and slicked back his hair.

Now, holding her close while swaying to a song, he whispered thanks to heaven that he'd given in to her request. The scent of her hair, the softness of her arms, the silkiness of her breath as it brushed his face, made the day disappear. All he saw was her.

He almost asked her if she'd taken back the letter she'd left in his room. With the return of his sight, he thought often of what it might contain. Instead of asking, he decided to wait and someday ask her to read it to him. If he had his way, they'd leave the hotel together in the spring.

He rested his cheek against her hair and closed his eyes. For the length of a song he could pretend she was his girl. "I think I created a string of unhappy hopefuls when I came down," he said as the song ended way too soon.

Betsy lifted her head and glanced around the room. "I'm not interested in any of them."

"Is there someone you're interested in?" With his finger, he tilted her face toward his. What if Betsy did have a fellow in the wings somewhere? Maybe overseas defending her freedom?

Her lips twitched. "Maybe."

A faster song started and he led her to a quiet table in the corner. "Are you thirsty?"

She nodded, a soft smile gracing her lips. "Water sounds wonderful."

He rushed to fetch her drink, wishing there was somewhere they could go that would afford them a little privacy. The temperature outside was too cold, not to mention the snow, and a secluded room would only tarnish her reputation. He'd been at the hotel long enough to know the rules regarding the waitresses' behavior. He filled two glasses with water from a pitcher and hurried back to the table before someone chose his empty seat.

"Thank you." She accepted the glass and drank.

Spencer forced his attention away from the way her throat worked as she drank, and focused on his drink instead.

"What changed your mind about joining the party?" she asked.

"Are you glad or sad that I came?"

"Glad, just curious." She raised her eyebrows. "You looked as if you'd had the worst day of your life."

"I did." He twirled his glass on the polished table. He debated how much to tell her, but since she was a regular volunteer at the hospital and no stranger to blood and disease, he decided to tell it all. "It's no secret I didn't want to have anything to do with doctoring the Germans."

"True." She stared at him with such intensity, he squirmed under her gaze. The lowered lights of the dining room made her flawless skin look almost ethereal.

"Do you know the young man named Schmidt?"

"Yes." She put a hand to her mouth. "What happened?"

"He died today." As much as Spencer held against the Germans, no one needed to die as the boy did, murdered. Someone had snuck into the infirmary and slit his throat. He'd been found by one of the nurses. The image had burned itself into Spencer's mind. Killing in a war, when bullets were flying in both directions, was one thing, but to kill a young man in his sleep, in the hospital, was barbaric and challenged everything Spencer felt toward the Germans.

"He was only seventeen." Tears shimmered in her eyes. "I wrote a letter home for him just last Sunday." She wiped her fingers across her cheek. "No wonder you were out of sorts. Is there anything I can do for you?"

"No." Leave it to sweet Betsy to be concerned for him. "The body is being prepared to be shipped home at the first opportunity."

"How many more have you lost to the flu?"

Good. He'd let her keep her assumptions. "Two." The other men were weak from their injuries. Spencer and Dr. Lincoln had done everything they could. It would have taken a miracle for them to live. "Dr. Cleary is recovering, so the wing is no longer understaffed. He helps out when things are slow with the American patients."

"Oh, that's good. I was feeling guilty about only helping once a week." She reached across the table and took his hand. "Thank you for helping."

He twined his fingers with hers. His still retained some of his summer tan while hers were as pale as the petals of an orchid. He was in grave danger of losing his heart. He dropped her fingers and straightened. "Care for another dance? I'm not much of one for the jitter bug, but the slow ones I can handle."

"I'd love to." She offered him her hand again.

He took it, a jolt of electricity shooting up his arm. Yes, he was a goner. Since there was no going back in his feelings for her, he might as well enjoy whatever attention she was willing to give him. He swung her into a foxtrot and promenaded around the perimeter of the room.

She tossed her head back and laughed, exposing the graceful line of her neck. He bent his head, ready to place a kiss under her jaw, and stopped. The intimate gesture could cause an awkwardness between them that would be greater than the time he'd stolen the kiss upstairs. He took a deep breath and shoved the urge deep inside him to explore at his leisure.

When the song ended, the lights came back to full capacity, signaling an end to the night's festivities. Gloria clapped her hands. "Don't worry guys and gals, we'll have more dances as Christmas approaches. Now, if you fine soldiers wouldn't mind helping us put the room back to rights, we'll all head up to bed soon."

"Looks like that's my cue to help." Spencer couldn't take his eyes off Betsy's lips. Before the war, a dance would end with a kiss from his date. Betsy's eyes widened, but she didn't pull back. Spencer lowered his head.

"Hey, move it, bloke. We've work to do." A soldier bumped his shoulder against him, pulling Spencer from

Betsy's spell.

He grinned. "Guess we'd better move." Was that a flicker of disappointment he saw in her eyes?

She sighed. "I suppose so." She started to pull away.

Throwing caution to the winds, Spencer yanked her back. Let the others wait. He claimed her lips and let the background noise fade away.

13

Betsy rushed into the infirmary, her arms filled with towels. A sad, haunting melody came from the far corner of the room. The same tune she'd heard come from Spencer's room a few nights ago. She sat the towels on a rolling table and went in search of the music.

Next to a bed containing a man with no legs, Spencer played his harmonica. Tears stung Betsy's eyes as she glanced at the patient. It wasn't the loss of his legs that was killing him, but the infection he'd got in his hand because he was too stubborn to trust American doctors after he'd cut himself.

Spencer sat in a hard chair, eyes closed, lips coaxing music from the metal instrument. Oblivious to anyone but the dying man and the music, he played "Amazing Grace" to ease the passage of the man into death.

Betsy leaned against the foot of the bed and forgot

the moans of the injured, the antiseptic smell of the hospital, and let her spirit soar with the music. Before long, she raised her voice in song.

The patients quieted, all eyes and ears on her and Spencer. As she sang one hymn after another, she strolled among the beds, straightening blankets, fluffing pillows, laying a cool hand against a fevered brow and relieving the men's discomfort wherever she could.

The hospital staff made their rounds with smiles on their faces and lessened worry lines. Steps seemed less hastened, voices less strident. Spencer played until the man took his last shuddering breath, then stood and covered the poor soul's face with a sheet. Without a glance at anyone, he marched from the room.

Betsy hurried after him, chasing him all the way outside. The winter sun did nothing to dispel the frigid cold and she shivered immediately upon stepping outside. "Spencer, wait."

"Go back inside. You'll freeze." He stared toward the tall fence circling the perimeter.

"What's wrong?" She placed a hand on his arm. "Did you know the patient?"

"No." He inhaled sharply through his nose. "He died from something easily treated because he hated us so much he couldn't stand for us to touch him." He glanced down at her with sorrow filled eyes. "I was no different. I looked at the Germans as something other than human, as monsters. I wonder whether I would have sought medical help under the same circumstances."

She wrapped her arms around her middle and hunched over against the cold. "No one knows what they would do under duress, but do you see what God is doing? He's healing you of your hatred."

"Or at least helping me disassociate from it." He led her back inside. "You shouldn't have followed me. What will we do if you get ill?"

The fact he cared warmed her more than the blanket he draped over her shoulders. "The flu has run its course. I won't be sick." They walked together back to the infirmary. "I hope you'll play your harmonica again. It calmed the patients."

"No more than your lovely voice. I'm sure they thought angels had visited." He tapped her nose and strolled down the aisle.

After folding the blanket she wore, Betsy headed to fill cups with water and assisted those to drink who couldn't help themselves. Peace still radiated from many of the faces. Hopefully, she could convince Spencer to start each Sunday afternoon off with music. If only for an hour, the differences between the Americans and the Germans could be eased and they could all come together to worship regardless of personal beliefs.

Whether the German patients believed in God or not, the hymns had provided them all with a measure of comfort. For Betsy, that was enough for now. Hopefully, she and Spencer had planted seeds of faith that would one day sprout and spread after the war.

"How in the world did you get Dr. Gregory to agree to help out?" Dr. Cleary stood by her elbow.

"I brought him in and let him see how much we needed him." Betsy turned with a grin. "How are you feeling?"

"Good. For a while there I thought the pneumonia would get the best of me. Doctors make the worst patients, you know."

She laughed. "I can imagine."

"I'm glad Gregory's sight allows for the prescription glasses."

"Do you think he'll always need them?" Betsy watched as Spencer made his rounds, his features once again set in determined lines, his shoulders square under his white coat.

Doctor Cleary shrugged. "There's no telling with head injuries. I can say, though, that he is a very lucky man." He winked and left, his footfalls echoing down the marble-tiled hallway.

*

It had done Spencer good to send the legless soldier into the hereafter with a peaceful smile on the man's face. It had also opened Spencer's eyes to a lot of prejudice still fermenting inside him. He wanted to look at the face of each prisoner as Betsy did—as a man, regardless of what uniform that man wore. But he still struggled to let go of the bitterness he held toward people who could so callously kill innocents; an army intent on eradicating a race of people from the earth.

He hung his dirty doctor's gown on a hook. It was an occasion to spend some serious time in prayer and meditation. He saw no other avenue for his peace of mind other than time spent in God's presence.

Then there was Betsy, the beautiful, kind-hearted woman who sent his senses spiraling and thoughts of his future whirling out of control. Just when he thought he couldn't love her more, she opened her mouth to sing. If his lips hadn't grown sore from the harmonica after an hour of playing, he could have continued forever just to hear her voice.

He had no idea what he wanted to do in a few months. And he knew her contract would be up, too. Did he want to pursue a discharge from the army and ask Betsy to marry him, or did he want to continue with the career he'd studied for? Could he be content as a civilian doctor? Would he miss the excitement and adrenaline rush of operating while under fire?

"Are you ready?" Betsy had her basket over her arm, her scarf around her head and a shadow of sadness across her face.

"What's wrong?" He crooked his arm while peering into her face.

"Nothing." Her shaky smile seemed forced.

"Is it too much for you to continue here? While you're invaluable, they can manage." If he saw signs of her overworking herself, he'd put a stop to her volunteering immediately. She already worked too hard as a waitress. The dear girl needed to take a break.

They trudged through the snow in silence to the car waiting to take them to the train. Spencer opened the door for Betsy, then slid in out of the cold. "Are you sure you aren't getting sick? You look pale."

"Of course I'm pale. It's winter." She pulled her coat tighter around her.

He continued to stare at her until their ride stopped. Once he had her on the train, a lap blanket across her, he pursued his questioning. "Something is going on in that pretty little head of yours, and I don't want to hear another nothing."

"Isn't a girl entitled to some privacy?" She turned her head away, but not before he saw the glimmer of tears.

"Did someone say something inappropriate?" He placed a finger on her chin and pulled her to face him.

She yanked away. "The men wouldn't dare. They love and respect me."

"Then what? Talk to me." Why couldn't she see that he cared about her? That it bothered him to see her so sad.

"Stop." She stood, the blanket falling to the floor, and moved to sit a couple rows in front of him.

The out-of-character action left him open-mouthed and staring at the back of her head. Usually he was the moody one, the person who wanted to be left alone.

The slump of her shoulders ripped at his heart. He'd leave her be until the train stopped, but he wouldn't rest until he found out what was bothering her.

"Got an ice storm coming," the conductor said as he came down the aisle. "This kind of weather keeps up and the trains will be stopped. Not enough people to keep the tracks clear."

Spencer thanked God for his warm room at the hotel. How many more days would he be able to make it to the hospital? What if he became snowed in on the base and couldn't make it back to the hotel? He rubbed fog off the window so he could peer out.

The winter wonderland, while beautiful, could dish out its own brand of death. Were the German prisoners able to keep warm enough? He knew they preferred cooking their own meals, which mostly consisted of their favorite food of potatoes, but were they supplied with enough fuel to run their heaters nonstop?

He wouldn't mention any of his concerns to Betsy. Knowing her, she'd strap on a pair of snowshoes and walk to the base to take them soup.

The train screeched to a stop, and he stood. Without talking, he held out his hand to help Betsy to her feet.

She offered him a grateful smile and accepted his hand. He still didn't say a word as they tramped through rapidly falling sleet to the hotel. Once inside, he faced her. "I will respect your privacy, but if I find out someone is harming you by either their words or their actions, I can't be responsible for what I'll do."

She cocked her head. "Oh, Spencer, you darling man, you are totally clueless to what might cause a woman to be sad." She patted his cheek and climbed the stairs, casting one last look over her shoulder before stepping out of sight.

Clueless? She was the one without a clue. What did Spencer have to do to make her see he was dizzy over her? Maybe he should have listened more when Ma tried to explain to him what made women tick.

"I'll tell you what's up, soldier boy." The head waitress grinned at him from the doorway leading into the restaurant. "That little gal cares for you a lot, and caring for you doesn't fit into her plans. When you can't see past the nose on your face to how she's feeling, it makes her sad."

"Should I go to her?" If having feelings for him made her sad, it might be better if he kept his distance. But what if, by doing so, she decided against caring for him? Love was too complicated. "What am I not seeing?"

"What are your intentions toward her?" She crossed her arms.

"I don't know." Other than thinking of when he could see her again, when he could steal another kiss, he hadn't asked her what she wanted. Before he could do that, he needed to know his own plans for the future.

"You need to figure it out before someone else grabs

her up." The woman pointed at him. "With all the men parading through here all the time, it won't take long." She spun, the ribbons of her apron bow flapping behind her.

Spencer rubbed his chin. She was right. He needed to figure it out. He headed to his room and opened the nightstand drawer. Running his fingers over the Bible there, he smiled. Ma had stuck the New Testament into his duffel bag the night before he shipped out. He'd always thought the book kept him safe. Now, he needed it for another reason.

He read until peace settled upon him like his favorite childhood blanket. He knew what he wanted to do in the future and strongly felt as if God had given His blessing. Now, all Spencer needed to do was talk to his Commanding Officer and talk to Betsy. What they said would cement his plans.

Tomorrow, he would visit his CO before heading to the infirmary. He kicked off his shoes and readied for bed. He couldn't wait until the time came to present his hopes to Betsy. Things would be rosy indeed if she agreed with his plan. After all, he was making them for her.

14

Gloria raced past Betsy, who had just left her room to start the day, and pounded on the other girls' doors. "Get up! Busy next few days. All hands on deck."

"What happened?" Betsy paused in the process of tying the bow on the back of her dress.

"Ice has the tracks unusable. A train full of soldiers and German prisoners will be staying here until the tracks are cleared. At least two days."

"Where will the prisoners sleep?" Betsy hurried after Gloria.

"Cots are being set up in the basement. The hotel has asked us to help serve the men their meals after taking care of the paying customers." She headed back the way she'd come. "I'm counting on you to help the most, especially since you have a heart for the enemy."

"Don't say that too loud." Gracious. Most people might not appreciate Betsy's beliefs. Look how long it had taken Spencer to come around to her way of thinking. "I'll be glad to help where I can. Even though it will be different to have them under our roof."

"Maybe you can get your handsome doctor to check them all over and make sure there aren't any pressing medical needs." Gloria winked and rushed away.

Bow tied, Betsy followed. In the dining room, busboys were busy trying to squeeze a few more tables into the already crowded room. The weekly dances might have to take place in the hall. She smiled, glad for any opportunity to serve, and shoved through the kitchen doors in search of the morning's most pressing chore.

Gallons of coffee would have to be made, and she proceeded to measure the grounds into large silver percolators when she heard the first raucous laughter of the train passengers. Different dialects floated through the door. It would be an exciting time with multiple countries represented under one roof. There would be little rest for any of the hotel staff that day and quite possibly the next.

"What has you so chipper on this winter day?" Chef Hooper stirred a lot pot of oatmeal. "Although that smile of yours sure does warm up a room."

"That's the oven." Betsy laughed. "I'm not sure why I'm so giddy. Maybe it's the opportunity to serve."

He shook his head. "There'll be no shortage of that. I'm making this pot of oatmeal for the prisoners before I start on the steak and eggs for the customers. We don't have enough supplies to feed the vermin with the heroes."

Betsy's smile faded. "I understand the need for simple food that can be made in large batches, but I do not understand your un-Christian mindset." She glared at the big man. In the past, she'd always thought his heart as big as his middle. She was wrong. "These are people fighting for what they believe in, the same as our men. They were possibly conscripted, just like our boys."

"Settle down, little girl." He waved his spoon. "Those *people* killed my two brothers. I'll cook for them, but I refuse to like the fact they're under the same roof as me."

"My grandfather died in a prison camp during the First World War." Tears welled. "He died because someone didn't care enough about him to dress a simple cut on his leg. If the so-called enemy had cared for him as God calls us to care for others, Grandpa might still be alive. If I can spare another human being that same type of misery, stop another family from mourning a senseless death, then I'll do what I can."

Spencer peered into the kitchen. "Betsy, what's wrong?"

She whirled, blinking back tears. "Just a disagreement between me and the chef."

"I could hear you out here." He stepped into the room.

"You heard me?" A lump formed in her throat. What if her views were made public? The soldiers would hate her.

"Not what you were saying, but the tone was loud enough."

"We were disagreeing on the matter of caring for the enemy being housed downstairs." Chef Hooper turned back to his food. "She's a German lover."

"That's uncalled for." Spencer's features hardened.

"Betsy, I'm sure you can find something to do other than help in the kitchen." He placed his hand on the small of her back and guided her from the room. "I understand your passion, and I did hear about your grandfather—"

She gasped.

"I was standing right outside the door because I was looking for you." He turned and put his hands on her shoulders. "What I'm trying to say is…while the prisoners are here, and we're overrun with allied troops as well, I think it prudent that you keep your views to yourself." He pulled her close and rested his chin on the top of her head. "Can you do that?"

She nodded, her heart swelling and fresh tears gathering. "Thank you for understanding."

"I'm starting to." He squeezed, then released her, holding her at arm's length and gazing into her face.

She could get lost in his eyes, so blue were they behind the gold rims of his glasses, so full of tenderness and compassion; she almost forgot she was hurt by his reluctance to verbally express his feelings for her. At times like this, she could almost believe he cared for her as more than a friend. That the kiss they'd shared held something more than just a moment of letting down their guard. She wondered if he would stay in Colorado after the snow melted and ask her to meet his family. Moments like this left her more confused than ever.

"I'll go make sure we have enough dishes set out." She pulled free from his embrace. "Thank you for calming me down in my moment of weakness."

"You aren't weak." He gave her a crooked smile that set her heart into flips. "You're one of the strongest gals

I know. You would have made a splendid field nurse."

She shuddered. "Heavens, no. I'll help where I can here at home." Being surrounded by blood and violence wasn't her cup of tea. She didn't mind helping in the hospital, even cleaning up after surgery, but she wasn't amenable to watching wounds sewed closed or bodies cut open.

She moved among the tables, making sure each setting held the proper dishes and utensils. So far, everything looked good. From the increasing noise outside the closed doors to the dining room, she guessed they'd be overrun in minutes. She glanced at the clock, saw that it was 7:00 a.m. and threw open the doors.

"Betsy?"

She stared into the brown eyes of Lloyd. Oh, no. She couldn't bear being confined in the same building as her former fiancé.

"Fancy meeting you here." He bent forward to place a kiss on her cheek.

She ducked out of his reach. He no longer had the right to kiss her, platonic or not. "Hello, Lloyd."

"You're still a looker." Lloyd's eyes roamed over her. "I never would have guessed you to be a waitress."

"Exactly what did you think I would do after you left me?" She crossed her arms. "This is a respectable profession that allows me to be of service."

He shrugged. "Thought you'd be married, is all."

"Hey, guys." Lloyd put his arm around a couple of the other soldiers. "This doll is from my hometown. We had a fling once upon a time. Isn't she a beaut?"

Betsy's face flushed. What had she ever seen in him? Had she been so desperate to follow in her friends' footsteps and marry a man fighting for her country that she'd jumped at marrying the boy next door? After all, Lloyd had done nothing but tease her growing up. He didn't seem to have changed much. What a blind, foolish girl she'd been.

Finally spotting Spencer across the room, she waved him over and slipped her arm through his. "I'd like you to meet my fiancé, Private First Class Spencer Gregory. He's a doctor."

*

Fiancé? Okay, Spencer would play along. He thrust out his hand. "It's a pleasure to meet you, Private."

"Likewise." His eyes narrowed as he glanced from Spencer to Betsy. "I hadn't heard you'd gotten engaged."

Her eyebrows rose. "Oh, kind of like I didn't hear you had gotten married until you returned home? Come on, dear, I need your help over here."

"You're a lucky man, Doctor," Lloyd called.

"I sure am." Spencer allowed himself to be led to the far side of the room. "Okay, what gives?"

"That's Lloyd Wilson, my…ex-fiancé."

"So? Why the charade?" Not that Spencer minded the other blokes thinking he was engaged to the lovely Betsy, but he wanted all the details.

"He arrived home on furlough with a foreign bride on his arm." A shadow crossed her eyes. "I didn't get a letter, a phone call—nothing to prepare me. I don't want him to think I've pined for him. He needs to learn a lesson. Will you help me? It will only be until the train pulls out."

Had she pined for him? Was that why she seemed to hold all the soldiers at arm's length, or was she truly one of the new generation of women who wanted a career rather than marriage and a family?

He studied her face, noting the way soft freckles dotted her nose, her blue eyes peered up at him, and the highlights in her hair caught the lamp's glow. No, Betsy was made for marriage. She was created to be a wife and mother. The fact she was single was an anomaly.

He wanted to ask her then and there to wait for him to be discharged. Uncertainty held his tongue. If he were sent back to the front lines after they were married, she would be left a widow. He wouldn't do that to her.

"Of course, I'll help you," he said, smiling.

"I was starting to wonder, you were quiet for so long." She frowned.

"Just staring into the face of the woman I'm going to marry."

"Great. You're playing the part well." She patted his shoulder. "I'll see you at the dance tonight."

"Another one?" That meant he'd have to share her attention.

"Of course. We'll need to entertain all these soldiers. Besides, we're all stranded here anyway. Oh, and the hotel would like for you to check over the prisoners bedded down in the basement." She grinned and rushed off to start work.

He groaned. Oh, well. Since he couldn't make it to Camp Carson for a few days, he might as well see what he could do for the poor souls downstairs.

Spencer chose a seat in her section across the table from Private Lloyd Wilson. He lifted his menu and watched the man over the top of it while his gaze followed the waitresses around the room. What a doll-dizzy soldier. Spencer felt sorry for the man's wife.

Betsy paused before taking the man's order, keeping a smile on her face as the girls were required to do. "Gentlemen, we've some hot oatmeal that will warm you on this cold winter day."

"Sounds good, toots." Lloyd smacked her bottom.

Betsy shrieked. Spencer leaped from his chair and reached across the table just as Betsy dumped a glass of cold water in the man's lap.

"Hey!" Lloyd jumped back. "What was that for?"

"I am not a thing you can pat or play with." She glared and tossed a napkin at him, then held up a hand to stop Spencer from ripping the man's head off. "I'm all right, Spencer."

He settled back in his chair, relieved that Betsy seemed able to take care of herself. Still, fire burned in his gut from the other man thinking he could treat her that way. Past love or not, he had no right to touch Betsy or any woman other than his wife in such a way. He rattled his menu and fought to control his emotions.

Betsy trailed her hand across his back on her way past, settling his temperature a bit but doing nothing for his emotions except send them rocketing. He got Lloyd's gaze and grinned. The other man had let a good woman go and now it was Spencer's turn to win her heart.

Private Wilson glared and stormed from the dining room. As far as Spencer was concerned, the fool could stay in his room for the duration of the ice storm.

After explaining who he was to the guard downstairs, Spencer checked the five prisoners in the basement and found them all healthy, although a little underweight. One of them was familiar to Spencer—eerily so. But with the dim light and his less-than-perfect eyesight, he couldn't place why.

The day passed with Spencer reading the newspaper, eating his meals and keeping an eye on Betsy. The only time he let her out of his sight was when he would go to his room for his daily bible reading. The day moved as slow as molasses running downhill in wintertime. He actually looked forward to the physical exertion of clearing the dining room after dinner to ready the room for dancing.

Once all the soldiers and guests crowded in, there was little space left to jitterbug, but when the music started, everyone forgot about the shortage of space. With the men outnumbering the women three or four to one, the women were danced to the point of exhaustion. Several of them kicked their shoes into the corner.

Spencer kept Betsy close. When men would ask her to dance, he'd shoo them away.

"I think you've played the part of doting fiancé long enough," she said. "I'm here for the others, too. A dance with them won't hurt."

He scowled. "As long as you stay away from your ex. I don't trust him."

"I have no desire to spend even a second with him." She whirled into the arms of a French soldier, leaving Spencer to dance with Gloria.

"So, when did you pop the question?" She wiggled her eyebrows.

"It's just pretense to keep another man from bothering her." He explained about Wilson. "Once the train pulls out, we'll go back to nothing more than friends."

"Pity."

The song ended, and he dipped her. "Why?"

She straightened. "I think she likes you more than she'll let on, but she doesn't trust a man in uniform. Seeing her ex here explains a lot. Bye, toots. Thanks for the dance." She sashayed away and into the arms of a staff sergeant.

Spencer leaned against a table and watched as Betsy laughed at something her partner said. If she didn't trust a man in uniform, that made it even harder for Spencer. The only way she'd accept his declaration of love was if he was able to get his discharge. But couldn't she see that not all service men wanted a different girl at every railroad station or in every country? They weren't all like Private Wilson. *He* wasn't like Private Wilson.

The subject at hand stared at Betsy as if she were a tasty plate of pie. When he caught Spencer watching him, he turned away and pulled one of the hotel's upstairs maids onto the dance floor. The ice wouldn't be cleared from the train tracks fast enough for Spencer. On the other hand, that meant the fun charade with Betsy would end.

He'd heard rumors that the hotel would be setting up a Christmas tree soon. He had no gift for Betsy. He might have to trudge through the snow into town or find a way back to the commissary on base. Maybe a necklace to grace her pretty throat.

"Hey, soldier, how about buying a girl a drink?" Betsy plopped into a chair next to where he stood.

"Sure. Coffee or water?"

"I sure wish we had some lemonade, but since we don't, water is fine." She smiled up at him. "Where were you? You looked very far away."

"Just thinking about Christmas."

"Missing your family?"

"That and other things." He left to fetch water for her and coffee for him. When he returned, he kept the subject on Christmas. "Where will the hotel get a tree?" It wasn't as if they could head to the woods to chop one down. Not with the amount of snow on the ground.

"I'm not positive, but I think I overheard someone say something about cutting one down on the hotel grounds." She shrugged. "It's better than nothing. I love Christmas, but I really haven't celebrated much the last few years."

"Why not?"

"No one to celebrate with. Lloyd was gone last Christmas, and I was alone the four years before that. I usually spend the day alone with my Bible and church service."

"I plan to remedy that this year." He'd make this her best Christmas yet.

15

"Since you love the Germans so much, you can take them breakfast." Chef Hooper motioned toward a tray filled with bowls of oatmeal and slices of toast. "The girl I had assigned to the duty is refusing."

Betsy sighed and straightened her shoulders. "I'll be happy to After all, even dogs need to eat, and the Germans are more than that." She glared at him before hefting the tray. "Other than what they believe, these men are no different than our own soldiers. God calls us to love all His children."

"Well, He didn't call me." The chef turned back to cutting out biscuits.

Betsy stifled a growl. She wanted to dump the oatmeal over the chef's head. Instead, she bumped the door led to the basement open with her hip. Normally dark, the basement was now illuminated with two dimly glowing bare bulbs. Careful to place her feet on each of the steep steps, Betsy made her way to the bottom and turned to give the guard a smile and a nod.

"Set it on that table," the young dark-skinned soldier said. "They'll fetch their own bowls. No sense in you serving them."

"I don't mind." She smiled and headed for the table. After setting the tray on the table, she turned to the five prisoners who shuffled forward, their hands and feet chained. "Do any of you speak English?"

"I do." A man with hair the color of wheat and blue eyes stepped forward.

"Do you have everything you need? Water, blankets, a deck of cards, maybe?"

He narrowed his eyes. "Why are you asking? Why not toss food on the table and leave like the other girls do?"

"Because for everything I do for you, I do for God."

"We do not—" he waved at his comrades "—believe in a God who loves everyone equally."

Betsy kept the smile on her face. "It doesn't matter. God believes in His creation. I'll return with your next meal." She gathered the dirty dishes from the previous night's meal and turned to leave.

"Wait. We would like the cards when you return."

Betsy nodded and brushed past the soldier, who watched their interaction without expression. She shrugged. It was no matter. Every word from God's Word planted seeds in those who heard it. Maybe the soldier's eyes would be opened.

She set the dirty dishes in the sink of sudsy water. Avoiding the smirk on the chef's face, she wiped her hands on a nearby cloth and headed for the dining room. Out of the chef's sight, she gritted her teeth. Oh, that type of thinking made her so mad!

"What's got your temper up?" Gloria wiped at a smudge on the counter.

"Stupidity for the most part." She glanced out the window. Snow continued to fall. "Any news on the train pulling out?"

Gloria shook her head. "Snow covered the ice. It's caused more problems. Maybe they will leave tomorrow."

Betsy frowned. Weariness washed over her. That meant at least one full day in the same building as Lloyd. It also meant another day of pretending to be engaged to Spencer. What was she thinking? Why hadn't she just told Lloyd that her fiancé was off at war? Because he might not have believed her, that's why. She'd do almost anything to keep him from thinking that no other man wanted her.

She propped open the double doors to the dining room. Once upon a time, the hotel had used a hostess to seat people at lovely round tables, but that was before the war made luxury take second place. She sighed at the long tables that made moving between them difficult. While the hotel still used white tablecloths and porcelain dishes, the effect lacked some of the prior glamour. She would have liked to have seen the place in its heyday.

"Hey, doll." Lloyd leaned in the doorway. "Where's your squeeze?"

"I'm sure he's in his room. Where's your wife?" She brushed past him to straighten a couple of crooked chairs.

"Back home waiting for her hero to return."

Betsy rolled her eyes. Hero, indeed. She thanked God

for sparing her the heartache of marrying Lloyd. She'd seen the hungry look he gave the waitresses last night. The man was a womanizer. Betsy felt sorry for his wife.

"Good morning, sweetheart." Spencer slipped his arms around her waist and kissed her cheek.

Surprised, she laughed uncomfortably and moved out of his embrace. "Not while I'm at work." Her stomach fluttered. Although it was only an act, the warm look in his eyes sent a flush up her neck.

"You never used to let me squeeze you in public." Lloyd pouted. "You barely let me kiss you."

"I guess it wasn't true love, Lloyd." She faced him. "Aren't you glad you realized that and married your French bride?" She smiled, caressed Spencer's cheek and dashed to the kitchen as if a swarm of hornets were chasing her.

Pretending engagement to Spencer had seemed like a good idea at the time, but now, she wasn't sure. What she did know was that the line between pretend and reality blurred. Despite her resolve not to, she was falling once again for a man in uniform. No, not falling. She'd already fallen all the way and it scared her right out of her no-nonsense white shoes.

Her hands shook as she carried a tray of water pitchers to the buffet in the dining room. Cups and saucers clattered like dice. What would she do if Spencer left? Could she let him go without a word? Her heart would rip in half. Sometime before spring, she needed to let him know her feelings. Maybe she could slip the letter she'd taken back into his room. It stated everything she felt and more.

"The prisoners' soup will be finished at one o'clock," Chef Hooper said. "You'll want to deliver it while it's hot."

"Yes, I will." But Betsy's thoughts were still on Spencer. Her heart skipped with ways she could tell him she loved him. She refused to let a sour-faced man bring down her spirits. Instead of retorting with a snide comment of her own, she headed to her table as a new rush of customers entered the dining room.

The day raced like a tornado across the prairie. By the time one o'clock arrived, Betsy felt exhausted and frazzled. Not only had it been hard work serving so many hungry men, but Lloyd also kept up his teasing about Spencer and her to the point Betsy thought she would have to step between the two men to avoid a fight. Sometimes she thought Spencer took their little charade a bit too far—like she did.

She pulled him aside after lunch. "You have to stop getting angry with every soldier that flirts with me."

"Your ex-boyfriend isn't flirting. He's disrespectful." Spencer crossed his arms and glared across the room. "I won't stand for any woman to be treated that way, especially my fiancée."

"We aren't really engaged," she whispered. Although she wanted to be, very much. What woman wouldn't want a man like Spencer defending her honor? "I need to go feed the prisoners lunch. You behave." She rushed to the kitchen.

Fragrant bowls of potato soup waited on a tray. Generous hunks of bread sat beside each bowl. "Why, Chef Hooper, they'll love this lunch."

"Makes no difference to me." He scowled and resumed stirring the huge pot in front of him.

"Of course it doesn't, still it's very kind of you to make something native to their tastes. God will be pleased."

"Humph."

Betsy laughed and lifted the heavy tray, happy with her tiny victory. "I can't wait to see what you prepare for dinner. You are a wonderful chef."

"Don't flatter me. Get down there with that food before they riot." He ducked his head to hide the grin that stretched his pudgy cheeks.

Betsy shoved the door open and felt for the first step, then the next one. Halfway down, one of the prisoners held out his hand for the tray. She missed the step. The tray went flying, and the floor rushed to meet her.

*

Spencer glanced at the dining room for what seemed like the hundredth time. Where was Betsy? The other waitresses seemed to be growing annoyed. There were too many customers for even one girl to go missing. He looked around and located Lloyd laughing with some of his buddies in the corner. At least that particular nuisance was occupied.

"Private First Class Gregory." The chef's voice boomed across the room. "Is he here?"

"I'm here." Spencer shoved back his chair and hurried toward the man. The chef whirled back to the kitchen, leaving Spencer to follow.

"Miss Colter has fallen." He motioned toward the stairs. "The guard cannot leave his station."

Spencer shoved past the chef and pounded down the stairs. Betsy lay on one of the cots. "Who moved her?"

"I did, sir." The Private stood at attention. "I didn't feel it was right to leave her on the cold floor."

"Get out my way, you fool." Spencer knelt beside Betsy. The guard could have caused more damage than the fall if she'd injured her neck.

Soup covered her uniform and coated her hair. A purple knot rose on her forehead. A gash over her eye bled into the pillow under her. "Tie up these prisoners and get me some ice," he ordered the private. "I can't tend her and guard them, too. Wait. Leave one able to help me."

His heart clenched. She looked so pale, so frail. He felt her pulse in her wrist. Steady but not as strong as it should be.

He smoothed her hair from her face. "I'm here, honey. I'm going to take good care of you." What were these fools thinking sending her down such steep stairs burdened with a heavy tray? Her determination to ease the discomfort of the prisoners could very well be the death of him, or her.

What was taking the man so long? "You." Spencer pointed at one of the prisoners. "Is there any water? A rag, maybe?"

The man nodded, said something to one of the others and headed for the table in the center of the room. The man he had spoken to stepped backward into the shadows. Spencer peered at him, unable to make out his features, and gave up trying to figure out what the man was doing when the guard returned. Behind him was one of the hotel maids, carrying several clean rags.

The guard carried a bucket of snow in one hand and a bucket of water in the other. "Will this do? It's all we have."

"It'll work. Thank you for thinking of it. Please move those men to the far side of the room to afford Miss Colter some privacy. You, miss, stay and help me." The best thing to do might be to move Betsy to her room, but Spencer needed to rule out any neck injury first.

After cleaning Betsy's wounds the best he could in a dark, dank basement, and determining that nothing was broken, he sent the maid to find some men to help him carry her upstairs. They could use one of the cots as a travois.

He washed his hands in the water left in the bucket and straightened to face the guard. "What happened?

"She was bringing the men their lunch, sir, and one of them approached her." The guard breathed sharply through his nose and stiffened his back. "She gave a cry and fell."

"Was she pushed?" It was an impossible thought. He turned to stare at the prisoners. "Did one of you push her? Is that what happened?"

"No. We would not harm her." One of them stepped forward. "She has been kind to us."

Spencer ran his fingers through his hair. He didn't know what to think. "Soldier, why didn't you see what happened?"

"Sir, it happened so fast. I glance toward the door and the next thing I knew—"

It was useless. He didn't see anything and the prisoners would never tell the truth. They knew what a hotel full of American soldiers would do if they found out one of them had harmed an American woman.

Lloyd and another man appeared at the top of the steps. "What happened to Betsy?" The lanky soldier raced down the stairs and to her side. "One of these Nazis hit her?"

"We don't know that." Spencer shook his head.

Lloyd lunged at the closest man, tackling him to the floor. Spencer and the guard pulled Lloyd off while the other soldier stood, silent and glaring.

"Get off me." Lloyd shook them off. "This isn't the end. I will find out what happened." He spit at the German's feet, then grabbed one end of the cot Betsy lay on. The silent soldier did the same.

Spencer followed them up the stairs and into Betsy's room. Once the two men placed Betsy on her bed, Spencer dismissed them and asked the maid to dress Betsy into her nightgown, and to let Spencer know when she was finished. He stepped into the hall and closed the door.

Lloyd and his friend whispered together at the end of the hall. When they spotted Spencer, they headed out of sight, taking the empty cot with them.

Spencer leaned his head against the wall and closed his eyes. When he'd seen Betsy lying on the cot injured, not only had he thought her grievously wounded, but it had brought back the nightmare of his own head injury. At least he had been at the hospital. Betsy wasn't so lucky. With the freak snow and ice storm, they would never make it to the hospital, base or civilian.

He prayed for God's intervention and healing. What seemed an eternity later but was only fifteen minutes, the maid opened the door. "She's ready for you."

"Thank you, miss. What is your name?" Spencer smiled at the plump dark-haired girl, who didn't look any older than eighteen.

"It's Molly. Would you like me to stay?"

"Please. It wouldn't be proper otherwise." He marched to Betsy's bedside.

"Sir, I have duties to perform. I can leave the door open a bit. That should suffice. I'll find the head waitress and let her know." At Spencer's nod, she did as she'd said and left him alone with the woman he loved.

He'd checked her vitals, bandaged her cut, and prayed. There was nothing more for him to do except sit by her bed and wait for her to wake up. He rested his forehead on the mattress beside her and listened to her breathe.

"Doctor?" Gloria placed a hand on his shoulder. "Go to bed. I'll sit with her now."

"What time is it?" Spencer wiped the sleep from his eyes. How could he have fallen asleep when Betsy needed him? He took her pulse again and watched the rise and fall of her chest under the cotton nightgown and heavy quilt. She looked as if she were sleeping, nothing more. He prayed she'd open her eyes by morning.

"It's too early in the morning."

"I don't want to leave her."

"Then let me have a cot brought in."

"I'll compromise and settle for that." He smiled and watched as she left, returning half an hour later with a tray of food, a pitcher of fresh water, and accompanied by two busboys toting a cot.

"You get some rest, Doctor. I'll check in on the two of you periodically."

When she had gone, leaving the door cracked open about six inches, he lay on the cot and folded his arms under his head. Betsy emitted a soft snore, bringing a smile to his lips. She'd be fine after a good night's rest. The Lord had been faithful in healing him and Spencer believed the Lord would heal Betsy.

Sleep eluded him now that he'd be awakened. He swung his legs back to a sitting position and reached for the water pitcher. He glanced toward the dresser. Sitting on top of it was a letter addressed to him.

Forgetting the water, he moved to the dresser. Could it be the one that had been on his dresser? The one that someone had taken? He glanced back at Betsy. Why would she take back her own letter?

He picked up the envelope, breathing in the faintest trace of rose water. Would she be angry if he opened and read it? After all, it was addressed to him. But then, she'd taken it back. Curiosity won out. He slipped a fingernail under the flap.

"Doctor." Gloria slammed open the door. "A gunshot in the basement!"

16

Why so much screaming? Betsy opened her eyes. Why did her head ache so much and why was she in bed? She didn't remember donning her nightgown.

Wait. She had taken a meal to the prisoners and fallen and hit her head. She felt the bandage near her temple. Spencer must have doctored her. She glanced at the chair beside the bed. The bright-colored afghan she sometimes curled up with was draped over the arm. Someone had clearly spent time recently in the chair. Spencer? Then where was he now?

Two maids thundered past Betsy's room. Why was her door open? She slid out of the bed, placing one hand on the bedpost to steady herself. She glanced at her uniform hanging on a hook. The commotion in the hall drew her like a magnet, but she didn't have the strength to get dressed.

She grabbed her robe from the foot of the bed,

slipped it on and tied the sash around her waist. She was as covered, if not more, than what her uniform provided. Taking small careful steps so as to not jar her head, she shuffled from her room and followed the yelling throng of people to the bottom floor.

"What's happened?" Betsy grabbed the arm of a girl racing past her.

"Gunshots in the basement. Something to do with a doctor and a prisoner." The girl yanked free. "That's all I know."

Doctor? Spencer? Her heart in her throat, Betsy continued to make her way through the crowd and into the kitchen. Several soldiers stood at the top of the basement stairs. They parted when they saw Betsy. The expression on their faces, some of judgment, others of shame, chilled her blood. Clutching the lace around the collar of her robe, she descended the stairs.

Spencer, gun in hand, stood over the body of one of the prisoners on a cot. Blood pooled on the cement floor a few feet away. "What did you do?" She asked, her voice hoarse.

"I didn't shoot him. One of these men did." He waved toward three men in a far corner. One of them was Lloyd.

"Why?" She did her best to walk straight as she approached Lloyd, but the pounding behind her right eye wanted to bring her to her knees.

"Because he hurt you. He pushed you down the stairs." Lloyd crossed his arms and glared. "Of course we'll make him pay."

"I fell. It was an accident." She turned to Spencer. "Tell them." When he shrugged, she turned to the guard. "You saw. I missed a step. It was no one's fault but my own carelessness."

"I didn't see anything," he said.

"Spencer, please." Tears trailed down her cheeks. "You need to help this man."

"I will." He shoved the pistol into the waistband of his pants and pulled her off to the side of the basement. "You shouldn't be down here. It's too cold, you aren't dressed properly, and you aren't wearing shoes."

She hadn't noticed the bitter cold on her feet until he said something. "I'm fine. That man is bleeding."

"I've stopped the bleeding. He needs surgery. I can't do that here."

"Can you move him to a bed upstairs where he will be more comfortable?" She gripped his arms. "He'll die down here."

"These soldiers will riot if we move him."

"It's a chance worth taking. A man's life—his soul—is at stake." Her voice rose as she pummeled his chest. "I thought you were different. I thought you were starting to care about what is right. If he stays down here, then so do I."

Already her feet were growing numb from the cold floor. She grew dizzy and swayed, reaching out for Spencer to steady her. Instead, he swept her into his arms and marched up the steps.

"You silly, tender-hearted girl." He held her close, the warmth of his body erasing the chill running through her. She wanted to be mad at him, she was mad at him, still his strength and caring for her felt wonderful.

"You need to make sure the prisoners aren't harmed any further. They're human beings, Spencer."

"I know, honey." He placed her on her bed and pulled the covers to her chin. "I'll send someone to sit with you."

"Promise me that you will care for that man."

He sighed. "I promise to care for him to the best of my ability."

"Thank you." She pulled the blankets tighter around her and closed her eyes.

When she awoke, weak sunlight streamed through her window. Finally, a small sign that the train would hopefully be able to pull out soon. She stretched and smiled. Maybe she could even venture out to purchase a Christmas present for Spencer to go with the letter she would give back.

Reality jolted her. What was she thinking? There was a man shot on her behalf downstairs who could be lying at death's door. She flung aside the blankets. Other than a dull ache, her head no longer throbbed. She hurriedly dressed in her uniform, shocked to see that it was nearing lunch time. Why hadn't Gloria awakened her?

Apron tied and hair in its customary bun, she dashed to the kitchen, relieved to see there was no longer a crowd gathered at the doorway.

Chef Hooper faced her. "The doctor gave the man some medicine and left to find someone to take him to Camp Carson so he could get some medical equipment. Your German will be all right."

"He isn't 'my' German, but I am relieved. What about the soldiers who shot him?"

"What about them?"

So it was to be that way. The soldier would go free. Well, not if Betsy found his commanding officer. She'd make a big enough stink for some type of punishment to be meted out.

"You don't need to worry about taking them food.

The head waitress has taken care of it."

"Wonderful." Betsy smiled. "I'll take it to them at dinner." She turned and pushed through the doors into the dining room. The winter sun shined brighter knowing that Spencer cared enough about her wishes to tramp through a wintery landscape to see them done. He truly was a wonderful man.

As if her thoughts had conjured him, he strode through the front doors, his gaze meeting hers. He grinned and held up a small black bag.

He must be frozen. Betsy returned his smile and hurried to pour him a cup of hot coffee. Mug in hand, she greeted him. "Thank you."

"Anything for my lady." He set the bag on a nearby table and accepted the coffee. "It's so cold out there, but the sun feels good."

"Did you make it to the base?"

"I did." He smiled. "I found a farmer with a sleigh. Took us a few hours, but we made it back safe and sound. I'm glad to see you up and about. How's the head?"

"Fine. A little sore, but not bad."

"Your eyesight?"

She cupped his cheek. "I see you just fine." Of course he would worry that her injury could leave her injured as severely as he had been. Through the grace of God, she'd only suffer a headache through the day.

He put his hand over hers. "I'm glad. If you could have someone bring me a sandwich and more coffee, I'll go see what I can do for our injured guest." He pulled back, retrieved his bag and headed for the kitchen.

Betsy wanted to take him his meal, but Gloria would

have none of it. She said she didn't want Betsy traipsing up and down the stairs until the next day. Sighing, Betsy asked one of the other girls to take care of Spencer while she waited the tables.

Every so often, she glanced toward the kitchen doors, hoping for a glimpse of Spencer or word on the prognosis of his patient. She didn't get either one as she raced from kitchen to table serving hungry soldiers. Whenever she got Lloyd's gaze, she glared, wanting nothing more than to dump gravy in his lap.

How could anyone think it okay to shoot a man in chains? A man unable to defend himself? Especially since none of the men involved had bothered to investigate to find out what really happened.

She had seen the battle going on inside Spencer when she'd gazed into his eyes. What if she'd been an hour later? Would he have let the wounded man die? Joined in with the violence of Lloyd and his buddies? She didn't want to think so, but the look on his face as he held the gun had chilled her.

She prayed for a quick ending to the war and mankind's hatred toward those who believed differently than they.

*

Spencer sat beside the injured man. He had looked familiar to him in the dim light of the basement. But during surgery, he'd realized something ironic…this was the same man who had caused his blindness. Now, he stared into the enemy's face. Obviously, God wanted Spencer to learn something from it all, but he hadn't a clue what. Forgiveness? Tolerance?

But what if this man had pushed Betsy down the stairs? What if she had been permanently injured because of it? Would Spencer have been able to keep his oath as a doctor to heal all? His shoulders slumped. He'd like to think so.

"How is he?" Betsy's voice wafted from the doorway of the small hotel room.

"He'll be fine." Spencer answered without turning, not wanting her to see the confusion on his face. Sweet Betsy would never think twice about helping anyone, alleged enemy or not. He held his hand behind him, beckoning her closer.

She slipped her palm in his much larger one and placed her other hand on his shoulder. "Have I ever told you about my grandfather?"

"No, not really."

She took a deep breath. "Grandpa came home from the First World War minus both legs."

"A landmine?" He wasn't sure he wanted to hear the rest of her story. Somehow he knew it related to her drive to care for the prisoners. He squeezed her hand.

"No. Grandpa was a POW. While tending the fields one day, his legs were cut on a wire. Not badly, but they got infected. Because he was the enemy, the German doctor in charge couldn't be bothered. When his legs got to the point that Grandpa was in great pain, a couple of the other prisoners helped him to the doctor. The doctor said the legs of an American were not important. He would have to wait.

"By the time the doctor got to him, it was too late and his legs had to be amputated." Betsy shuddered. "When the United States entered into this war, and the opportunity came to minister at Camp Carson, I took it. Why should another family have to suffer as mine did because of prejudice? Why should another injured man fighting for what he believes in, whether we think it right or wrong, not receive comfort? That is not who God called us to be."

"We can't all be like you." Spencer stared at the carpet between his feet.

She played with the hair at the nape of his neck, sending shivers down his spine at her touch. "You're more like me than you know." She planted a kiss on his cheek and glided from the room.

He shook his head, tired of the charade. For a few minutes, it was if they were two people in love, instead of a man in love with a woman who only playacted. He wanted to call her back, tell her his feelings, find out how she felt about him. Gloria had said once that Betsy wouldn't fall in love with a man in uniform because of Lloyd's betrayal. Spencer needed to somehow show her he was nothing like the other man.

"That is a good woman." The German opened his eyes and stared at Spencer. "I am surprised you have not killed me, while I once tried to kill you. I know you remember."

Spencer shrugged. "I took an oath, and as a doctor, must follow that oath."

"But you hate me."

Spencer raised his eyebrows. "I cannot call you a friend, that's for sure."

The man laughed, then winced in pain. "Maybe someday, after this war, we will meet again on the street of some fine city and exchange a smile in greeting. Does God not talk about forgiveness?"

"He does." The man's mentioning God surprised Spencer. Maybe Betsy's sweet nature and strong faith were having an impact. He glanced toward the window.

The sun still shone, and the far-off whistle of a train blew. "Looks like you'll be sleeping in the hospital at Camp Carson come nightfall."

Spencer stood. "I'll look in on you on Monday." He was ready to take the next step beyond volunteering. He was going to ask to be stationed at the base and be assigned to the prisoner wing of the hospital.

Spencer could no longer fault the young man lying on the bed for his temporary blindness. He had been frightened, and retaliated out of that fear.

After leaving the room so the patient could sleep, he went to see whether the trainload of stranded soldiers had a chaplain among their ranks. To his delight, the front desk clerk told him a pastor was a civilian guest of the hotel and was enjoying a late dinner in the dining room.

Spencer found the grey-haired man alone, reading the newspaper with a hot bowl of chicken noodle soup in front of him. "Sir, may I have a moment of your time?"

"Certainly." The older man folded his paper and motioned for Spencer to sit beside him. "I'm Chaplain Anderson. What is bothering you?"

Spencer wasted no time in telling about his initial reluctance to help the German prisoners and why he now wore glasses. He also spoke of the identity of the prisoner he had operated on a short while before. While Spencer talked, the pastor sat quietly, his hands folded on the table, and kept his gaze locked on Spencer's.

When Spencer finished, the pastor sat back and said, "That's quite a story. How do you feel now?"

"Confused, but I've decided to actually request that I be assigned to the hospital rather than request a medical discharge. I have no desire to head back to the front lines. I don't think I can be in a situation where I might have to pull a gun on another man."

"Any other reason?" Pastor Anderson's mouth twitched, and he glanced over Spencer's shoulder.

Spencer turned. Betsy stood at the end of the table, her face lit up with a grin. "I believe there might be," he said. "But she doesn't like military men, not in a romantic way at least."

"I think you're wrong." The pastor placed a gnarled hand over Spencer's. "Talk to God and read His Word. Follow His leading. Perhaps, it will also lead you to that gal's heart—and something much more."

The train whistle blew again. Pastor Anderson stood, folded his newspaper and gave Spencer a nod. "I'll be praying for you."

When Spencer stood, he noticed the small bag in Betsy's hand. "Are you leaving?" His heart sank. He had been so worried about receiving a transfer of his own it had never occurred to him that she might.

Her misty gaze lifted to his face. "I'll be gone until Christmas Eve. I'll be riding the train for a few days, serving the soldiers there."

He smoothed a few loose strands of hair from her face. "What about your head? Do you feel all right?"

She leaned into his touch. "I'm fine, although I'll miss you."

"Will you?" He wrapped his arms around her waist and pulled her close. "I don't want to pretend we're engaged anymore, Betsy." He rested his cheek against her hair. "I want—"

Lloyd cleared his throat next to them. "Train is leaving. Don't worry about your gal, Doctor, I'll take good care of her."

Every ounce of Spencer's being tensed. He pulled back, shaking his head, and studied Betsy's face. She smiled, and tilted her head as if to tell him, *There's nothing I can do.* He expelled a sharp breath and tapped her nose. "Be careful."

"I will." She kissed her fingers then placed them across his lips, and then she left, leaving the room cold despite the fire roaring in the fireplace at one end of the room.

The moment she returned, he would express his feelings for her and not let anyone stop them. He didn't care if every guest and staff member of the hotel heard him. In the meantime, he'd find the perfect Christmas gift for her. But what did one buy the woman of his dreams?

He headed to the train platform, unmindful of the cold that immediately seeped to his bones, and watched as Betsy climbed the stairs to the train. She glanced back and blew him another kiss, causing hope to bloom in Spencer's heart that maybe their charade wasn't a charade for her, either. After all, Lloyd was leaving. There was no more reason to pretend.

In another car, soldiers loaded the prisoners, a couple of them carrying the wounded man on a stretcher. He lifted his hand in farewell to Spencer. Spencer returned the gesture, then turned to seek Betsy's face through a window. He found her three windows back.

She had written three words in the condensation on the glass. "Read my letter."

17

Betsy waved a last goodbye to Spencer. The moment Gloria said one of the regular waitresses on the train had fallen ill and that Betsy would have to take her place, she had retrieved her letter and replaced it on Spencer's dresser. Her heart beat as fast as train wheels turned as she imagined his reaction.

Would he return her feelings of love? She thought so. Only a fool could not see the softening in his gaze when he looked at her or sense the heat of his kiss. Instinct told her that the ardor of his kisses were more than the lust of a lonely soldier, that they were founded in love. The knowledge had been cemented when she'd heard his words to the man in the dining room. The bitter Spencer was gone, replaced with a tender, more compassionate one. A man that Betsy felt safe giving her heart to.

Gloria had said the train would stop for the night in

New Mexico. Maybe Betsy could find Spencer a Christmas gift. Something that conveyed how much she loved him. A token reminder of their friendship that had, hopefully, blossomed into something more.

"It's a tragedy, that's what it is." Lloyd plopped next to her. He placed his arm along the back of the seat, tickling her neck with his finger.

She scooted against the window and slapped his hand away. "What is?"

"That your fiancé can't come along." Lloyd waved out the window as Spencer shrunk smaller and smaller as the train pulled away.

"He's a busy man." She put her hands against his chest and shoved. "Get back. I'm no longer your girl."

"That, too, is a pity." He pulled a cigarette from his pocket. "So much has changed since you left home."

"You married a stranger while engaged to me."

He shrugged. "True, but she only wanted to come to America. I was a gentleman and obliged. We got an annulment soon after."

"You mean she saw your true colors, as I have." She moved to the seat across from him. How could she have thought herself in love with him enough to marry him? He was not a tenth the man Spencer was.

"Don't be that way. I'm a free man now. We can go back to what we were." He grinned, the freckles she had once thought cute now making him look like a naughty boy with a mean spirit. "After all, I did defend your honor with those Nazis."

"So, it was you who shot that man." She crossed her arms and glared. "I would never marry you, Lloyd. Never."

"Fine. Marry your German-loving doctor. You're

suited to each other." He flicked the ash from his cigarette on her shoe. "Shouldn't you be serving us men food?"

"Meal service doesn't start until we leave Colorado Springs." She wiped the ash with her finger, leaving a grey smudge against the white. She sighed, not sure why she felt the need to defend herself.

"I'll go sit where the girls are friendlier."

"Wonderful idea." Betsy waited for him to leave then headed for the dining car. If she stayed where she was, he would only come antagonize her again.

The dining car looked like a small restaurant, and because of its small size, Betsy would push a cart up the aisles of the passenger car containing the soldiers. Undoubtedly some would complain about the box lunches after the finer meals they'd eaten at the hotel, but everyone made sacrifices at war time.

"You must be the substitute. I'm Greta." A woman as tall as most of the men Betsy knew greeted her. "Your job will be easy, if you can avoid the groping hands some of the soldiers have." She winked. "I bet you can handle them, though."

Betsy resisted the urge to groan. "I've fought off my fair share." She glanced out the window as they stopped at the base for a few minutes. The hospital rose in the background, and she wondered about her prior patients and how they'd fared with her gone.

"Got a beau?" Greta's question drew her back to the dining car.

"Back in Colorado Springs. He's a doctor in the Army."

"Stationed at Camp Carson?"

"Not yet. He's recovering from an injury." Betsy

stacked the brown boxes containing the men's lunches on the cart. "I'm going to propose to him when I return."

Greta snickered. "You're going to propose? Good for you. Sometimes the men wait too long."

"All I need now is the perfect Christmas gift." With the cart full, Betsy was ready to go.

"There's a bookstore in Santa Fe. They sell books and wonderful gifts. Some are silver-plated despite war rationing. I'm sure you can find something there."

"Thank you." Betsy gripped the handle of her cart and headed toward the passenger car. She could handle a week on the train. Already it looked easier than the hotel, and she could definitely use the break. Add in the fact she had access to a store where she could purchase Spencer a gift, and she entered the passenger car with a spring in her step.

While Lloyd continued to tell ribald jokes, the rest of the men were courteous and respectful. Betsy ignored her immature ex and kept a smile on her face while she did her job.

"Hey, aren't you the girl who was helping the Germans? My buddy was their guard." One of the soldiers glowered. "Yeah, you're the one that took them their food every day and was overheard preaching to the chef about how they're people just like us." He threw his box at her, striking her in the shoulder. "Well, I don't want your food."

Before she could react, two strong hands gripped Betsy's shoulders and moved her aside. Spencer lunged forward and hauled the man to his feet. With his nose inches from the other man's, he promised to knock his lights out if he ever talked to his girl that way again.

Spencer tossed the man back into his seat and turned to Betsy with a grin. "Hey."

"Oh, what are you doing here? How did you... I saw you on the platform." She gripped his hands. "How—"

"Well, technically, I'm still on medical leave and not under the regulations of active duty. A trip sounded like just the thing. I got on when the train stopped for fifteen minutes at Camp Carson. A buddy of mine gave me a ride in a jeep. It was cold."

He'd come for her. Obviously, he couldn't bear to have her out of his sight. "I'm sitting in the front if you want to find me when you're finished here."

Had he read her letter? Was that why he was there? She took her hands off the cart and clasped them in front of her. A joy almost too powerful to contain filled her as she rushed through handing out the rest of the boxes. Maybe once the men settled down to sleep, she and Spencer could have a long-awaited heart-to-heart.

She hurried back to the dining room and up to Greta. "He's here."

"Who?"

"The man I'm going to marry. He got on at Camp Carson."

"He followed you?" Greta squealed, her wide mouth stretching into a smile. "How romantic. Show him to me?"

They peered through the small round window in the door of the car. Greta drew in her breath and fanned her face. "He's a looker, all right. A doctor you say?" At Betsy's nod, she giggled. "Maybe I'll suddenly take sick."

There hadn't been a lot to laugh at since the war and Spencer's injury, but having him follow her to the train released months of giggles inside her that came tumbling out. "Hands off, sweetheart, he's mine." Or he would be one day soon.

"Lucky girl." Greta grinned and turned back to her work. "If you find another one like him, send him my way."

With her work finished until dinner time, Betsy headed to the car where Spencer waited. She sat next to him and stared into his sleeping face. Poor man. He must have been up late tending the injured prisoner. Settling back onto her seat, she stroked his hand, content to sit and stare at the man she loved.

She spotted the letter she had written him sticking out from his pocket. On the pages she had spilled her heart, telling him how much he was coming to mean to her and how much she looked forward to his return. Then, she'd heard nothing, and he had returned a broken man. Now, here he slept, healed and better than before.

Her words on the page were few, but she hoped they conveyed her feelings.

When dinnertime came and still Spencer slept, Betsy wondered whether he was ill. When night came and he still hadn't awakened, but had stretched out to lie lengthwise along the seat, and snores emanated from him, she located two blankets and spread one over him, wrapping the other around her.

If he was going to stay there, she would, too. Her sleeping bunk would be there the next night. She kept her gaze trained on his face through the dim lighting until sleep overtook her.

*

Spencer opened his eyes and smiled to see Betsy

asleep across from him. Why hadn't the silly girl slept in her bunk? The girls were given sleeping berths; there was no need to sleep on the harder bench seats. Still, knowing she slept a mere foot or so from him warmed his heart.

Someone toward the front of the car shouted. The train lurched and screeched to a halt. Spencer lunged forward to catch Betsy before she rolled to the floor.

"What happened?" She blinked, her face inches from his.

He almost pulled her into a kiss. Instead, he helped her back to her seat. "Stay here. I'll go check." He cocked his head. "I mean it. Stay here. If it's something dangerous, I don't want to have to worry about you."

She pouted, but stayed seated. Spencer rushed forward, pushed along by the throng of soldiers all fighting to see what had stopped the train.

He stepped outside and was slapped by a bitter wind that threatened to take his breath away. An engineer dashed by. "Come on, men. We've a downed tree to move."

Spencer shivered and dashed back for his coat before jumping to the ground and following the man. A massive tree lay across the tracks, its bare limbs devoid of leaves but heavy with ice.

The engineer tossed him an axe. "Thanks. The sooner we get to chopping, the sooner we can move."

Spencer caught the axe and swung. Its blade bit into the frozen wood and jarred his arm all the way to his shoulder. Soon, despite the cold, sweat poured down his back. He prayed he wouldn't take sick. Not when he was so close to telling Betsy of his true feelings.

"I hope there aren't more of these," said a man on his

right. "I'm frozen to the bone."

"If there are," Spencer said, "then we get out and chop that one, too." He glanced up as Betsy and a woman almost as tall as his six feet strolled toward them bundled in blankets and carrying pitchers.

"Coffee!" Betsy held up her pitcher and thrust a hot cup at him. "Take a moment to warm a little." She removed one of the blankets from her shoulders and draped it, still warm from her body, around his. The lovely, smiling giantess did the same for another man.

It took almost two hours for them to clear the track, chopping the massive tree and moving the logs. The physical exertion kept them from freezing to death, that and Betsy's blanket, coffee and smile, but Spencer still thought the cold would never leave his bones by the time he reentered the train car.

"Here." Betsy handed him a key. "Head to my bunk and get those wet clothes off. Warm up your feet. I'll leave extra blankets and coffee outside the door."

"I can't take your bed."

"Yes, you can. Go." She gave a shove against his back. "You need a hot bath, but we don't have that. This is the best we can do."

His teeth chattered so bad, he couldn't argue. He hurried to her berth and shed his clothes, wrapping a blanket around his shivering body. Betsy's letter! He searched his clothes. It was gone. Lost outside in the snow.

The train started to move, erasing any hope Spencer had of finding it. He hung his wet uniform on a hook. What would she say when she found out he had lost it? He dug in his bag for his warm pajamas. He donned them and peeked out into the hall.

Spotting Betsy coming toward his room with a tray, he ducked back inside. When he heard her footsteps fade, he opened the door wide enough to bring in the tray of hot coffee and soup, along with a note from her stating she would see him in the morning.

He stared at the note, wishing it was the letter, and imagining what the letter might have said. Had it been a declaration of love or something awful? Maybe it was her way of breaking off their friendship. No, the look on her face had been tender, not resigned. It couldn't have held bad news. She loved him, he knew she did. He didn't need to read it on a sheet of scented stationary.

He brought the note to his nose and inhaled the slight traces of her fragrance. Betsy would understand. It was his heart that would ache for a while since he couldn't add her latest letter to the pile he'd brought home with him. He'd ask her what it said. That would be better. This way, he could gaze into her eyes as she told him the words on the paper.

When she finished, he'd ask her to be his wife. That's what he would look for in El Paso. An engagement ring as pure and precious as Betsy.

He set the idea of a ring aside and dug into the cooling soup. By the time he had finished, there came another knock on the door. Opening it, he discovered an extra blanket. He would be as snug and comfortable as man in the comfort of his home.

The next morning he dressed and headed for the dining car to catch a glimpse of Betsy. She was busy stacking a rolling tray with boxes of breakfast.

"Good morning," he said.

She straightened. "Good morning. You look much

better."

She didn't. The dark circles under her eyes gave testimony that the train seats left a lot to be desired as a bed. "You shouldn't have given me your berth."

"I wanted to. You're too tall to spend hours sleeping on these seats."

"The other men did."

"You aren't the other men." She smiled and patted his cheek. "Have a seat. Greta will fetch you something hot for breakfast."

"You can't keep pampering me. I'll eat what the other men do." He followed her into the passenger car.

Lloyd wasted no time in making a snide remark about the special treatment some people got. Betsy whirled and pierced him with a sharp gaze. "If you had gone out and helped chop that tree, instead of staying warm and cozy in here, maybe someone would have cared to make your night a bit easier." She dropped a box in his lap and continued past him.

Spencer grinned and chose a seat at the front of the car. They'd be arriving at their destination before the noon hour, and he had a very special errand to do. Once he purchased the perfect ring, he would ride the rails with Betsy until it was time for her to return to Colorado Springs.

Then, he'd speak with his commanding officer about that discharge. Spencer was willing to settle anywhere Betsy wanted. He'd go to the frigid Alaskan tundra or the deserts of Arizona. As long as she was beside him, the location didn't matter. He could be a doctor almost anywhere.

"Goodness." Betsy plopped into the seat across from him. "While the work might be easier delivering box lunches to the soldiers, I'd prefer to have my feet on solid ground again. I wonder if I'll walk straight when we get off."

He chuckled. "You follow God's leading wherever you go, Betsy. Your paths will always be straight."

"Aren't we philosophical this morning?" She bent and refolded her ankle socks to their proper position. "I'd love a pair of silk stockings. I miss them. Oh, and a pound of sugar to be used in any way I wish."

"The war won't last forever. You'll have those things again."

A broad smile lit up her pretty features. "And won't we spoiled Americans appreciate the luxuries more? At least for a week or two." She rested her head on the back of the bench. "I'm exhausted."

He patted the seat beside him. "Sit here. Use my shoulder for a pillow."

"It won't be proper, Spencer." She glanced around them. "It's broad daylight."

"I'm tired of propriety. Come."

She practically flew across the small space between them and nestled close under his arm. As her breathing evened out, Spencer thanked God for the precious gift of Betsy.

18

Her week of substitute duty over, Betsy enjoyed being back in the familiarity of the El Otero. Maybe she wasn't so adventurous after all.

"Betsy."

She turned away from the stack of plates to face Spencer. With a pale face and pained expression, he looked like a man haunted or one who had received bad news. She ran to him and wrapped her arms around his waist. She stared into his face. "What is it? Is it your parents?"

"No." He held her at arm's length. "I've been to see my commanding officer."

"Yes." She bit her lips, eager to hear what he had to say, and yet more frightened than she had ever been. Today was Christmas Eve. What could possibly have Spencer this upset?

"Can you get away for a few minutes so we can

speak in private?"

Were there complications from his head injury? How could that be? He rarely used his eyeglasses anymore and never complained of headaches. If not that, what could possibly have him looking as if death tapped on his shoulder?

Gloria gave her permission to spend a few minutes in the common room upstairs. Being the middle of the day, the girls should all be working and the room empty.

Once inside, Betsy tossed propriety to the wind and closed the door. She grabbed Spencer's hand and tugged him to the sofa. "Tell me."

"I got my orders. I'm being shipped out…to France."

"When?" Her heart stopped. She placed a hand over the spot on her chest where it should beat. "What about a discharge?"

"They denied it. I'm healthy and capable of active duty. I leave in the morning."

On Christmas? It could't be.

He gripped her hands. "I wanted…" His eyes grew misty, bringing tears to Betsy's eyes. "This isn't how I wanted to do this." He pulled a small black box from his pocket. "I want to marry you. I know how you once felt about military men, but I believe those thoughts no longer matter. Please, Betsy Colter, will you be my wife? Will you wait for me?"

She shook her head, the tears flowing freely now. "No. I won't wait for you."

He pulled free and started to turn away.

"Wait. I won't wait for you, Spencer, because I want to marry you. Now. Tonight. Before you go. I can't bear for you to leave me again, but if I'm your wife, I'll stand bravely until you return."

"What will you do? I could be gone as long as a year or more." He pulled her to him, almost crushing her in his strong arms. "You won't be able to continue working here."

"I'll figure out something. All you need to do is worry about coming home safely to me. Where can we get married on such short notice?"

"The chaplain on base will marry us." He stood and pulled her to her feet. "Are you sure you want to do this?"

"I'm more sure than I've ever been about anything in my life. Let me tell Gloria where we're going. I want to change my dress." This wasn't how she'd envisioned her wedding to be someday, but when Spencer returned, they could have a proper wedding with his family and friends in attendance. Right now, all they needed were each other and God's promises.

Two hours later, they stood in front of the army chaplain, Betsy in a light blue dress and Spencer looking dashing in his military dress uniform. She hardly heard the words of the chaplain, so deeply was she focused on Spencer's face. Oh, God, protect him. Bring him back to her.

"I now pronounce you man and wife."

Spencer bent to kiss her, his lips warm and firm against hers. She deepened the kiss, putting all her fear and love into that one kiss. If this were to be one of the last, she wanted it to be a kiss that would live with her forever.

He wrapped his arms around her and crushed her to him, burying his face in her neck. She didn't know when the chaplain left them, only that when Spencer ended their embrace, they were alone in the army chapel.

"I rented a room at the hotel," Spencer told her. "Do you mind if we stay there until the morning? I don't want to share you."

She tried to smile through her tears. "I'd like nothing better."

The ride back to the hotel was made in silence. While their hands remained linked, Betsy and Spencer sat in worlds of their own. She wasn't positive what went through her husband's mind, but she battled the oppressive spirit of fear. Surely God wouldn't have brought them this far only to take him away from her.

She studied Spencer's profile. His eyes were closed, his long lashes, too long for a man, still damp from his tears and casting shadows on his cheekbones. She raised a hand to caress his face.

His eyes snapped open. He pulled her close, still not speaking, and rained kisses upon every inch of her face, lingering on her eyes and the corners of her mouth. Oh, how she loved him.

In their hotel room, Betsy perched on the bed, a small wrapped package beside her. The diamond from her wedding ring winked at her. She had never received a better Christmas gift than her ring and her husband.

Today, she was married. Tomorrow, she would be alone. "Spencer, sit with me."

The bed sagged under his weight. "Yes?"

"I bought you something in Santa Fe." She handed him the package tied up with red and green ribbons. "I had no idea how much comfort this gift would bring me until now."

He unwrapped the box and lifted the lid. "A silver

pen?"

She shrugged. "It's engraved, *With all my love, Betsy*, but that isn't the gift I'm talking about. I bought the pen for your career as a civilian doctor. Something nice to sign your prescriptions with. Unwrap the other thing in the box."

He unwrapped a small Bible. "The New Testament."

She blinked back tears. "It will fit in your pocket. I signed it and slipped a photo of myself inside. Now, you can take me and God with you. It will help me, knowing that you carry God's word so close to your heart."

"This is the best gift I've ever received. I promise to never let it out of my sight." He wrapped the Bible in tissue paper and set it on top of his folded uniform, ready for his departure in the morning. "I'm going to ask you to keep the pen in safekeeping. When you are missing me, remember how much I love you and that I will be thinking of you each second of every day." He sighed. "I lost the last letter you wrote me. What did it say?"

She smiled. "I'll write you plenty more, but that letter said only three words... *I love you*. Nothing more, just those three words and my name. When spring arrives, someone will find that letter and read of my love for you. Maybe it will bring a smile to their face."

"How could you still love me after the way I treated you when I arrived back? Is that why you took it from my room?"

She nodded. "You were broken and wounded. For a while after your return, I admit I thought you were like the other men, a different girl in every city and all that, but as God worked on your heart, I realized I still believed those three words I had written you. I just had to wait until God finished refining you. Once I realized that, I put the letter back."

"You are one of a kind, Betsy Gregory." He kissed her.

"I like the sound of that," she said. "Betsy Gregory."

"If I'm not home when the snow melts, go to my parents." He pulled her into his arms, resting his chin on the top of her head. "Tell them who you are and show them our marriage license. They'll welcome you with open arms and give you a home. I don't want to worry about how you're supporting yourself."

"Okay." She smiled and stood. "Enough talking, husband, time is racing by."

The next morning, Betsy fought back tears as she waited with Spencer on the train platform. She didn't want his last sight of her before he shipped off to be one of her face red and her eyes swollen. "I'll write every day," she promised.

"I'll write as often as I can." He put a hand on each of her shoulders and stared into her eyes. "Each night when you lay your head on your pillow, remember how much I love you." He gave her a crushing kiss and stepped back as the train conductor gave the signal to board. With a wink and a wave, he bounded up the steps.

She followed his progress as he passed each window until he chose a seat in the back. He placed his palm flat against the glass. Betsy ran alongside the train as it pulled away, keeping her eyes on Spencer for as long as possible.

*

"My dearest husband," Spencer read the first of

many letters as he sat in a corner of the medic tent and did his best to ignore the gunfire and exploding shells bursting in the distance. The mail had been slow and he received a bundle of mail rather than one precious letter at a time. He planned to not move until he'd read every letter and prayed God would hold off sending him wounded until he filled up on Betsy.

> The Harvey Company agreed to let me finish out my contract even though we got married, so I'm employed until January. I've spoken with your parents on the phone and they can't wait to meet me, same as I am excited to meet them. Until the pass is cleared, I will work in the hotel gift shop. Don't worry about me. God is providing. You take care of yourself.
> Love,
> Your wife.

He opened the next letter.

> Dearest husband,
> I know the mail is irregular, but I'm aching for a letter from you. I need to know you're safe.
> I have news I believe you will be pleased to hear. You're going to be a daddy. Our child is due in the fall. Are you pleased?"

Spencer gripped the letter tight enough to crumple it.

He was going to be a father. He flipped the envelope over and read the postmark of February. He sighed. It was now March. Had she gotten his letter saying he'd be home sometime late summer? He might miss the birth of his first child. It helped knowing that God was watching over Betsy and the unborn infant. And when Spencer did return home, his duty was complete. He'd never have to leave her again.

He had just read the last letter, postmarked a month prior, when the casualties started pouring in. Spencer spent the nighttime hours doctoring the wounded and praying with the dying. At first, he had actually been skittish as each casualty was brought in. But as time passed and he spent time in the New Testament, which never left his pocket except when he was reading it, God healed him from the nightmare of his last tour of duty.

Now Spencer kept his focus on returning home to his wife and child. He had just made the last soldier comfortable when a prisoner of war was brought in, escorted by three American soldiers. "This one has a bullet in the side," one of the soldier said. "Be careful. He's a little upset with us."

Déjà vu. Spencer motioned for them to lay the injured man on the table. "Do you speak English?"

The man nodded, his face twisted in pain.

"Don't try any funny stuff with me. I'll doctor you up as good as new, but I'm the one holding the needle here. Understand?"

The soldier grinned. "I understand perfectly. The needle can go in easy or the needle can go in hard. I, too, am a doctor in my country. This why I give your men a hard time. There are others in more danger than I of dying."

Spencer chuckled and gave the man a shot of morphine. "I'll see to them, too. Our medics do their best to assess the casualties before they're brought in. I'm sure you needed the attention first. You've been shot."

"Bah." The man waved a hand. "Not the first time. My wife...she will be very angry with me. Says to stay out of the way of the bullets. Wait until she finds out I have been captured. She will be furious."

Spencer laughed out loud. Oh, Betsy would love this guy. He would have to write and tell her as soon as the rush of wounded stopped.

This time last year, he would never have thought to write of the war and the wounded. His letters had been more about how he felt about coming overseas and how much he missed Betsy's smile. Genuine letters, but fluff compared to what he wrote now. Now...he spilled his emotions across the page like a flooded river. Now...he shared his experiences with her, rather than just writing about them.

"Aren't you afraid of being captured?" Spencer cut the man's uniform away from his body.

"*Nein.* I've heard the Americans are good to their prisoners. They even let us eat potatoes and cook for ourselves. We can work in the fields if we do not want to sit idle."

He was mostly right. He probed the wounded area, eliciting a hiss from the German doctor. "The bullet has passed all the way through. I'll clean it and sew you up. You'll be as good as new."

"I say this to the men who brought me. They take me over man with broken leg. Pah. Fools."

Spencer would have enjoyed spending more time with the funny man, but others waited for his attention. Maybe, God willing, they would meet again under different circumstances. Who would have thought last year that Spencer would even contemplate a friendship with a German soldier? God worked in miraculous ways, softening even the hardest of hearts.

After the wounded stopped trickling in, and before catching what little sleep he could, Spencer took the time to write Betsy of the German doctor and the wife who would be furious as her husband's carelessness in getting captured. He could picture Betsy's smile and hear her throaty laugh. He glanced at her picture propped against the lamp.

While the photo stayed inside the Bible, he pulled it out when he wrote to her. It made him feel as if she was beside him and they were carrying on a conversation. When he'd finished the letter and sealed the envelope, he turned off the light, grabbed the picture and stretched out on his cot.

*

On September 10, Spencer did not want to stop at the El Otero Hotel. Betsy was no longer there. He wanted to hurry to Camp Carson, find a jeep and race his way through Rabbit Ear Pass and into the arms of his wife. A bit more than nine months had seemed more like nine years.

He stayed on the train while others disembarked and remembered the very first kiss he had shared with Betsy. The time she had given him the handkerchief he still carried in his pocket. Did she know that? He couldn't remember if he had ever told her he still carried it.

By the time he got to Camp Carson, his nerves twanged and he paced like a child waiting for Santa Claus while someone fetched him a jeep. When the jeep arrived, so did Dr. Cleary.

"Dr. Gregory." He held out his hand. "We're sorry to see you go. I had hoped you would be transferred here when you returned Stateside."

Spencer returned his shake. "No, sir. I'm a civilian now. I want nothing more than to see my wife and child. A civilian doctor will be just fine for me. No offense, but I'm in a hurry."

"I know you are."

"I will. Thank you. I'll return the jeep in a day or two." Spencer slid behind the wheel and set off through the pass.

When he pulled into the yard of his parents' house, he sat and stared at his childhood home and the beautiful woman waiting on the front porch. In her arms, she held a precious baby wrapped in a blue blanket. Tears sprang to Spencer's eyes. He soaked in the sight for a few minutes before climbing from the jeep.

The moment his foot touched the gravel driveway, he ran. Betsy met him at the bottom of the stairs. Spencer wanted to swing her into his arms and cover her face with kisses. Instead, he kissed her and then gazed into the sleeping face of his son. "I am a blessed man."

"Oh, Spencer, I've missed you so." Betsy rested her head on his shoulder. "You've missed so much being away."

"There will be other babies." He gave her a squeeze. "As many as you want. I'm going to set up a practice here in Colorado, if that's all right."

"That sounds perfect. Your parents will be happy. They're waiting to see you."

"They'll have to wait." He wanted to see them, too, but the other half of his heart came first. He needed to gaze into her eyes until his heart became whole again. That might take a few minutes of holding her. "I love you." He kissed her again.

The sun came out from some high clouds and shined upon them as if God himself were smiling and saying, "It is good."

* * * * *

DEAR READER

Dear Reader,
Camp Carson, now Fort Carson, held thousands of WWII prisoners. It was also a training camp for nurses, cooks, tank battalions and a Greek infantry battalion. Pack mules were a common sight, carrying supplies over the mountainous terrain.

The camp was not known to be anything but humane to the almost 9,000 prisoners, mostly Italian and German. Since it was within a reasonable distance to the El Otero hotel and Harvey Restaurant, I enjoyed exploring the possibility of a Harvey Girl and a wounded soldier coming to terms with what God would want us to do when facing our past pain.

For Betsy, it was a drive to prevent senseless injuries to prisoners. For Spencer, it was overcoming bitterness. I hope I was successful in showing how God can heal our hearts through any circumstance.

I took some liberties with the weather and played a bit with the train schedule and distance from the hotel to the camp. Forgive me if I strayed too far, but this is the fun of writing fiction. I hope you enjoyed this tender love story between Betsy and Spencer.

Fondly,
Cynthia Hickey

Don't miss the other Harvey Girl stories:
Guiding With Love
Serving With Love
Warring With Love

ABOUT THE AUTHOR

www.cynthiahickey.com

Cynthia Hickey is a multi-published and best-selling author of cozy mysteries and romantic suspense. She has taught writing at many conferences and small writing retreats. She and her husband run the publishing press, Winged Publications. They live in Arizona and Arkansas, becoming snowbirds with three dogs. They have ten grandchildren who keep them busy and tell everyone they know that "Nana is a writer."

www.ingramcontent.com/pod-product-compliance
Lightning Source LLC
LaVergne TN
LVHW012018060526
838201LV00061B/4363